# THE STILLMAN CURSE

**Peggy Morse**

## A KISMET™ Romance

**METEOR PUBLISHING CORPORATION**
Bensalem, Pennsylvania

Sisters. We shared the same parents, the same genes. We grew up in the same home, the same environment, yet we each developed into uniquely different individuals. Many times it was those very differences which kept us close, binding us throughout the years with an invisible cord of friendship. Sisters. Friends. I cherish both relationships we share. Although physically I stand a good three inches taller, I always find myself looking up to you. Lynne, this one's for you.

Special thanks to Dr. and Mrs. Dean Carpenter, and Ken and Melanie Hemry for knowledge shared while I researched the medical and legal questions raised during the writing of this book. To Ben and Butch McCain for allowing me to fictionalize the lives of some very real "characters." And to Nancy Deaver who willingly—well, almost willingly—attended a Bachelor Auction with me and made sure I went home empty-handed.

## PEGGY MORSE

Peggy Morse . . . an avid reader before becoming a published writer, Peggy believes in romance and its importance in our daily lives. The author of four published novels, she received the Romantic Times Bookmark of the Year award in 1989 and made the Waldenbooks Bestseller list in 1991. Known for her strong characterizations and skill in visualization, Peggy's main goal in writing is to offer the readers a good story, one they'll remember long after the last page is turned.

# ONE

Leandra Gallagher couldn't for the life of her figure out
where this blue mood had come from, but she wished it
would disappear. Ever since awakening, she'd had the
most absurd premonition of approaching doom. *How ridiculous*, she thought as she marched barefoot across the
bricked porch to the driveway circling the front of the
estate.

Dressed in a nightgown and chenille robe, she stopped
and glanced up at the sky, shielding her eyes against the
bright early morning sunshine to study the billowy clouds
suspended overhead. Birds twittered a cheery morning
song from the branches of the redbud trees bordering the
property at her right. A long satisfied sigh escaped her. It
was much too pretty a day to be wasted wallowing in the
doldrums.

Determined to shake off the unwanted mood, she whistled an accompaniment to the birds' song as she scooped
the morning paper from the driveway. With two quick
rubs, she peeled off the rubber band wrapped around the

thick roll of newsprint and flipped the paper open to expose the front page. She strolled back to the house scanning the headlines, pausing only long enough to push the front door closed with the ball of her foot.

Across the cool marble floor of the entryway she padded, crossing under the dining room's double archway as she made her way to the kitchen without ever glancing up from the paper. She'd made this journey every day for over eight years and could do it blindfolded if necessary.

In the kitchen she poured two cups of hot coffee, liberally lacing one with cream before she retraced her steps across the marble entryway. Circumventing the front door, she crossed into the living room, juggling the two steaming mugs while securing the newspaper against her side with the weight of her elbow.

She placed one mug on the coffee table to the right of a cloud of pipe smoke she knew to be John and received a grunt acknowledging the courtesy. Smiling, she settled herself on the sofa and divided the paper in half, giving the sports, business, and front-page sections to him, while keeping the women's, food, and real estate sections for herself. After propping her feet opposite John's on the coffee table, Leandra took a cautious first sip from her mug before shaking open the women's section.

She scanned the page, her gaze settling on the picture that covered the bottom half. Her fingers clutched convulsively at the newspaper while panic clawed up through her chest, slipping its bony fingers around her throat and slicing off her breath.

*Oh, God, no!* she thought as she squeezed her eyes shut to block out the half-page spread. Images and scenes flashed like laser beams through her mind, hurtling pain-filled memories from the past into the present.

She forced her eyes open and looked again. The tension

her fingers drew on the paper created taut waves across the photograph dominating the front page of the women's section. Pictured in vivid color were five women in evening dresses grouped around a tuxedoed man seated on the hood of a Rolls-Royce. It wasn't the women or the Rolls that held Leandra's attention. It was the man.

The fact that she hadn't seen him in over eight years didn't prevent her from recognizing him. Every detail of his face had been burned into her memory long ago, never to be forgotten.

One palm pressed flat against her pounding heart, Leandra read the headline—BACHELOR AUCTION TO BENEFIT BALLET—then quickly scanned the accompanying article until her eyes settled on his name. *Robert Todd Stillman II returns to Oklahoma City in time to offer his services as one of the bachelors to be auctioned in Saturday night's gala benefit for Ballet Oklahoma.*

*Back to Oklahoma City? Oh, God, please no!* Frantically, she searched the remainder of the article but found nothing to hint at the reason for his return.

"Something wrong?"

Startled by the sound of John's voice, Leandra dropped the newspaper to her lap. She saw the concern in John's eyes and quickly masked her hurtling emotions. "No, why?"

"I thought I heard you groan."

"Did I?" She waved away his concern with a casual flip of her hand. "It must have been this sale advertisement I saw for a pair of shoes I paid full price for."

John rolled his eyes heavenward and shook his head, muttering something about women before he turned his attention back to his paper.

The lie, even if it was just a little white one, left Leandra feeling guilty, for she owed John so much.

For eight years they had shared their mornings in this same way—sitting opposite each other in comfortable silence, their feet propped up, nursing their first cup of coffee of the day while reading the morning paper.

Now that she thought about it, the pattern extended back farther than her time with John. Even as a little girl in her parents' home, she remembered spending Sunday mornings this way. Her older brother had delivered the Oklahoma City paper in their hometown of Tecumseh, and many a Sunday morning she'd watched the sun rise over their neighbor's rooftop while helping Joe, Jr., roll the newspapers and wrap them with rubber bands.

In exchange, Leandra would receive a paper of her own. She would read it from front to back, never missing a word, but always saved the women's section until last, like a dessert, studying the latest fashions, reading about the wonderful parties, looking at the beautifully decorated homes, . . . and dreaming she was a part of it all. Dreams were all she had then. With eight brothers and sisters there hadn't been money for much else. A quick glance around the formal living room that she relaxed in reminded her how much things had changed since then—at least for her. Moiré drapes and Aubusson carpets were quite a step from the crisp muslin curtains and worn linoleum of her parents' home.

Moisture filled her eyes, and Leandra fought back the most ridiculous urge to cry. What was wrong with her today? She was becoming positively maudlin!

With a quick sniff she gave the paper a firm snap, forcing her attention away from the picture of Todd Stillman. She focused instead on an ad announcing a fur sale at Koslow's and another for a trunk showing of Bill Blass's fall collection at Balliet's. As she had done so many times in the past, she dealt with the unwanted memories by pushing them far back into her mind.

Making a mental note to check out the showing at Balliet's, she flipped the page. But it was no use. She closed the paper and dropped it to her lap, a deep sigh escaping her. The dark shroud of melancholy she'd been fighting all morning at last slipped over her. She glanced at the newspaper lying in her lap, then picked it up again. *So this is it*, she thought as she looked at the handsome man pictured there, *the return of the prodigal son*.

Her fingers dug into the thin paper, crinkling it in her fist as an unfamiliar emotion seeped into her, slowly replacing the unexpected shock of having seen him again.

Revenge. She wanted revenge. After eight years of harboring only a deep-seated resentment, Leandra Gallagher suddenly wanted more. Smoothing her hand across the wrinkled picture, she realized fate had just dropped the means to achieve it in her lap.

"Damn fool."

Sure that in some way John had discovered her vengeful thoughts, Leandra glanced up at him in surprise. But he was absorbed in his own section of the paper, half-glasses perched on the end of his nose, his lips puckered out in a frown.

His grumpy look distracted her from her own thoughts and drew a smile. "And what are you frowning at so early this morning?" she teased.

"Humph," he said as he hit the newspaper with the back of his hand. "Fools. All of 'em are fools."

Laughing softly, Leandra moved to stand behind him and draped an arm across the back of his chair. Accustomed to his crotchetiness, she riffled her fingers through his thick shock of white hair before leaning forward to peer over his shoulder at the paper. "Who's a fool today?"

"Just look at this!" He snapped the paper out and pointed a long finger at an even longer list of bankruptcies. "Fools. All of 'em. Spending money like it was water on things they had no use for. Just because they had it to spend. Should have used some sense and put some back for the bad times."

Leandra laughed and hugged him to her. "Not everyone is as smart as you, John."

"Damn right! If they were, they'd still have money tucked away and wouldn't be wondering where their next meal was coming from."

"Speaking of meals, I need to start breakfast." She planted a quick kiss on John's cheek, then straightened, pulling the belt of her robe tighter around her waist. "I'm going upstairs to get dressed. Do you need anything before I go?"

"No, no. Go ahead," he said, shooing her away before turning his attention back to the list of bankruptcies.

As she climbed the stairs, Leandra could still hear him muttering to himself. The oil boom may have made John Warner a rich man, but it was his own sound business savvy that had protected him when the price of oil had dropped, bankrupting so many of his contemporaries.

As her bare feet sank into the thick nap of the Oriental rug that ran the length of the upstairs hall, Leandra's thoughts drifted from John to the Bachelor Auction and the picture of Todd Stillman. By the time she reached her bedroom at the north end of the long hall, the need for revenge rolled like a lead ball in her stomach.

She crossed immediately to the country-French armoire standing between two floor-to-ceiling windows. She swung open its heavy doors and pulled out the bottom drawer.

Tucked beneath her winter sweaters was secreted a small wooden box. Dropping to her knees, Leandra opened the box's lid and sifted through several documents before finding the piece of paper that had drawn her there.

Folded neatly into thirds, the blue paper had faded to gray along its edges. With shaking fingers she smoothed the creases open against her thigh and looked at the rectangular paper she hadn't touched or even allowed herself to look at in over eight years.

All the pain, the humiliation, the regrets she'd felt then flooded back to wash over her again. Hot tears stung her eyes and blurred her vision, making it impossible for her to read the scrawled lines of handwriting. But it wasn't necessary for her to see the words again. . . . Every one was engraved upon her heart.

The band around his neck grew tighter and tighter, threatening to cut off his air supply. Hanging must be a hell of a way to die, Todd thought as he struggled to work a finger between his neck and the tight band circling it. There would be those awful moments of suspense in which a person had to face the reality of his own death before his body succumbed to the lack of oxygen.

He again tugged at the band of white choking him and silently damned his sister Ellen for getting him into this mess in the first place.

He glanced down the row at the other nineteen men who lined the narrow hallway outside the main ballroom of Oklahoma City's Marriott Hotel and mumbled another frustrated oath. Dressed in tuxedos, they all looked like a bunch of penguins on parade.

Without knowing yet quite how, he vowed to get even with his sister for volunteering him for this. Just because *she* enjoyed serving on the board of every civic and charity organization in Oklahoma City didn't mean the rest of the family had to get involved . . . especially him!

Out of nowhere a bird-like woman dressed in a bright yellow dress appeared at his side and started chirping. "Okay, boys, it's almost time for us to begin. Now remember, this is for charity, and we want those ladies to pay big prices for you, so smile pretty."

A tall, ruddy-faced man, wearing a red cummerbund and standing about halfway down the line, made some lewd comment that was followed by a burst of nervous laughter from the men standing near him. The woman, whom Todd had mentally tagged "the canary," opened the door a crack and peeked into the ballroom. From behind her, Todd caught a glimpse of the crowded room.

Women dressed in sequins and silk sat around small round tables that framed the T-shaped ramp. Beyond the tables was row after row of chairs. Probably the "cheap seats," Todd thought irritably. He remembered Ellen's mentioning that the ladies who purchased seats at the tables closest to the ramp paid a premium for the privilege.

While thinking he had never seen so many women in one room in his life, he heard his name called from the podium's microphone at center stage. It was his signal to begin. The instructions during the practice earlier had been specific: walk down the red carpet stretched between the rows of chairs, climb the four steps to the ramp, walk to the far end of the top of the T, then back to the center, stop, turn, walk to the tip of the T, stop, turn, walk back to the center, then stop and wait for some woman to buy him. It was humiliating.

His face burned in embarrassment as he approached the ramp. Now he knew how livestock felt when they were led into the auctioneer's ring. Hearing his vital statistics read over a PA system to a crowd of gawking women had to be the epitome of humbling experiences.

"Ladies, you won't want to miss bidding on this one. Bachelor number one is six feet two inches tall, has black hair and gray eyes, and weighs one hundred eighty-five pounds. He is thirty years old, and his astrological sign is Aquarius."

*Who the hell cares what my sign is?* Todd thought as the mistress of ceremonies—whom he recognized as a local television personality—droned on while he made the required circuit mapped out for him. He tried not to think about the hundreds of gaping women. Instead, he focused on a spot on the wall just above their heads. It was a trick he'd learned in a college speech class years ago, a bit of trivia he'd figured he'd never need to implement.

He'd already decided what type of women to expect at a function like this. The mathematician and scientist within him had joined forces to neatly categorize them and file them alphabetically in his mind with a list of accompanying characteristics. They all had two traits in common: they were oversexed and desperate. Otherwise, why would it be necessary for them to "buy" a date?

"And who could pass up a date package like this?" the mistress of ceremonies gushed. "An exotic stay in Ixtapa, Mexico." She paused dramatically while murmured oohs and aahs floated around the room. "The trip begins with the arrival of a chauffeured limousine at the home of the highest bidder to take our couple to Will Rogers Airport. From there they will board an airplane and jet away to Ixtapa, Mexico, for three nights and four days of romantic fun."

*Mexico!* Already aware of the mistake he'd made in allowing his sister to talk him into this farce, Todd panicked when he heard the date package his sister had arranged broadcasted by the MC. Three nights and four days in a foreign country with a complete stranger? What had he been thinking when he'd agreed to this . . . this nightmare?

By the time he reached center stage the first time, he'd worked himself into quite a state. His mouth felt like it was filled with cotton and his smile like a crack in weathered concrete. A rivulet of sweat slowly worked its way down the center of his spine, and he flexed the muscles of his back in an attempt to stop the irritating sensation.

After making the required turn, he headed for the bottom end of the T, finding it now impossible to ignore the women's excited whispers, the occasional catcall, and even—God help him—a few laughs as he walked the length of the ramp.

He was going to kill Ellen just as soon as he got off this stage.

The entire walk took four minutes, max, but to Todd it felt like an eternity before he reached the top bar of the T again. At this point, an auctioneer—probably borrowed for the night from some cattle auction—commandeered the microphone and began his chant. Todd's newly discovered kinship to cattle and horses grew as he listened to the fast-talking auctioneer. He felt like a pedigreed bull or some high-powered thoroughbred stud put up on the ring for sale.

A burst of movement in the audience caught Todd's attention. He watched in amusement as a man wearing a cowboy hat, ruffled shirt, tails, and a bow tie jumped up on a chair to serve as a spotter for the auctioneer. Todd couldn't help but laugh when he saw that the man was dressed in a tux only from the waist up. From the waist down he wore denim jeans and cowboy boots.

A lady from the "cheap seats" yelled out, "Fifty dollars!"

"Fifty-now-a-hundred-who'll-give-me-a-hundred? Fifty-now-a-hundred . . ." Words rolled off the auctioneer's tongue faster than blood from a severed artery.

*Fifty dollars*? Beads of sweat popped out on Todd's forehead. What if no one else bid on him? What if he brought the lowest amount? God, how demeaning! This auction had to be some woman's idea. No man in his right mind would make a fellow man go through this kind of hell.

A bleached blonde, who had undoubtedly been melted down and poured into her black silk jumpsuit, hopped up from her seat at one of the front tables, waved her number, and shouted, "I'll give a hundred dollars!"

"Hundred-now-two-who'll-give-me-two? Hundred-now-two—"

Worried he'd bring such a low price, Todd forgot his earlier nervousness and began to scan the audience for some sign of interest. His gaze met that of a woman sitting almost directly at the end of the ramp. Immediately, his view of the women who attended these functions took a hundred and eighty–degree turn. This woman was a knockout!

She was alone, which was odd since three or four women occupied most of the other tables. As she sat beneath one of the massive crystal chandeliers in the ballroom, her black sequined dress shone with a dark pearlescence, rivaling the sheen of coal-black hair piled high on her head.

Thinking he could maybe pull a bid from her, he broadened his smile and gave her a wink. A beam of light from the chandelier glanced off the diamond ring on the lady's left hand as she discreetly raised her card, exposing the number one hundred and sixty. In a split second, the auctioneer's spotter was at her side. She whispered something in his ear, and he shot his arm up with three fingers held high.

The auctioneer yelled out, "Three hundred dollars! Now-we-got-three . . ."

Puzzled by the big jump the woman had made from the last bid, Todd continued to watch her. While everyone else seemed to be laughing and having a good time, this woman was cool, calm, and collected. The rings on her finger suggested she was married, but he knew one of the rules governing the auction was that only single women could bid. Maybe the lady was divorced or widowed.

A shiver chased down his spine as she continued to stare at him. Whooee! but she was a cold fish. He'd handled cadavers in medical school with more warmth than this woman exuded. He offered a silent prayer that the ice queen would be outbid.

It seemed his prayer was answered when, not to be outdone, the bottle blonde jumped up again and shouted, "Four hundred dollars!" The ladies at her table laughed and clapped their hands, offering their friend encouragement as she sank back down on her chair, holding her breath while waiting to see if her bid would hold.

The spotter turned expectantly to the ice queen. Without removing her glacial gaze from Todd's, she lifted her card again and tapped it twice.

The auctioneer bellowed, "Eight hundred dollars!"

Eight hundred dollars! Damn! The woman had just doubled the last bid. The crowd went wild. People were laughing and yelling while uniformed waiters bustled from table to table, gathering cocktail orders obviously in hopes the ladies' tips would be as exorbitant as their bidding.

"Nine hundred."

*Now this is more like it*, Todd thought in smug satisfaction when he heard a bid called from the opposite side of the room. The bid came from his right, but when Todd turned to see who'd placed it, his elation slowly disintegrated.

The woman holding her numbered card aloft was old enough to be his mother. In an apparent attempt to make herself look younger, she'd piled on about three inches of makeup and dyed her hair a rusty shade of red. Her dress was cut low enough to expose a generous amount of cleavage of which she was obviously proud, judging by the way she leaned forward, offering Todd a better look while she batted false eyelashes at him.

Swallowing hard, Todd offered the aged Lolita a weak smile before looking away from her and straight into the eyes of his laughing sister. At his steely look of entreaty, Ellen laughed and pointed to her wedding ring and mouthed, "Sorry. I can't bid."

"Ladies, ladies, la-a-dies," the auctioneer implored. "Surely we aren't going to let this man go for a mere nine hundred dollars. Did I mention he was a doctor? Think what you'd save in medical bills alone! Come on, what do I hear? I've-got-nine-hundred-give-me-ten-who'll-give-me-ten?"

"Nine fifty," yelled the bottle blonde. She grabbed a pen and started scribbling furiously on a piece of paper. Todd wondered if maybe she was doing some fast figuring to see how high she could afford to go. He was tempted to slip her a blank check. Compared with the other two bidders, she seemed the lesser evil.

"One thousand," the geriatric Lolita called.

"One thousand!" echoed the auctioneer. "We've got us a hen fight for sure. Which one of you ladies wants to spend a weekend in Ixtapa, Mexico, with the Doc? Huh?

Who'll it be? I've-got-one-thousand-who'll-give-me-two-I've-got-one-who'll-give-me-two-two-two-two-who'll-give-me-two?''

The blonde looked nervous. Her friends leaned to her, whispering advice. She pressed her fingers to her temples, shook her head, then stole another look at Dr. Robert Todd Stillman II. The battle waged within was clearly etched on her face.

Todd ignored the ice queen and turned a reluctant eye back to Lolita, silently praying she was out of the action. Unfortunately, the woman held in her hand a roll of bills that would choke a horse and was silently mouthing numbers as she thumbed through them.

The auctioneer was playing this to the hilt. He gave each of the ladies a meaningful look. ''I hear he's a heart doctor, ladies. Now wouldn't you just loooove to have your pulse checked by him?''

''Two thousand!'' As soon as the words were out, the blonde clapped her hands over her mouth.

''Two thousand! Who'll-give-me-three-two-who'll-give-me-three? Come on, girls, don't let opportunity pass you by. I've-got-two-who'll-give-me-three?''

Anticipation crackled in the air as the auctioneer paused dramatically. ''I've-got-two-two-I've-got-two. Two thousand dollars. Goooooing once. Goooooing twi—''

''Five thousand dollars.''

For a split second, silence hung like a heavy curtain over the room. Heads strained to see who'd made the bid. Whispered questions buzzed around the room. ''Who is she? Do you know her?''

''Five thousand dollars!'' the auctioneer roared as he sliced his arm down with the speed and accuracy of an executioner, sealing Todd's fate. ''Sold, to the little lady in black, number one sixty!''

Thunderous applause shook the ballroom while Todd forced his gaze from the bottle blonde to the ice queen. The woman lowered her chin and angled her head slightly, her eyes narrowed in a look of smug satisfaction.

*Well, that's that*, Todd thought as he walked off the stage. Bought and sold like some hunk of meat out of the butcher's window to be delivered to a living and breathing freezer. He stopped at the foot of the stairs and pulled a single red rose from a crystal vase there. The only thing expected of him now was to give the woman the rose and get her check. Then it was over.

Well, almost, he thought ruefully, as he remembered three nights and four days in Mexico.

"Great job, Todd."

He forced a smile and nodded at the compliments as he made his way through the crowded room toward the round table at the foot of the ramp and the ice queen who awaited him.

As he approached, he saw she was watching the stage and listening intently as the second bachelor was introduced. What was she going to do? Buy another one? The woman obviously had more money than sense.

Todd glanced up at the stage and stopped to watch the second bachelor make his way down the ramp. This guy was smooth. As he strolled—if you could call it a stroll, it came damn close to being a swagger—down the stage, he looked from side to side, making eye contact with women on his left, then on his right, and smiling a secretive smile at each. Midway down the ramp, he stopped, slipped his hand into his pocket, and withdrew several Hershey's Kisses. He tossed one of the foil-wrapped chocolates to a lady on his left, then one to a redhead on his right. The audience loved it. Bids started flying from all sides. Spotters were running back and forth, trying to keep up with the action, while the auctioneer's chant echoed around the room.

The smile building on Todd's face slowly dipped into a frown when the bachelor eased to the foot of the stage, his gaze centered on the ice queen. Taking another Hershey's Kiss from his pocket, bachelor number two pressed it lightly to his lips and tossed it to her. She caught it in her hands, laughing gaily. When he lifted an eyebrow inquiringly at her, she smiled but shook her head. With a shrug of disappointment, he turned his attention back to the redhead.

Surprise and, maybe if he was honest, even a little jealousy surged through Todd. The ice queen hadn't even smiled once at him during his time on stage, and she'd bought him! How did the candy man manage to finagle any sign of warmth out of the woman?

Well, Todd Stillman had as much charm as the candy man. The ice queen just hadn't experienced its devastating effect . . . yet. With that comforting thought, he approached her table.

"Hi. I'm Todd Stillman." When she turned to face him, he saw she was even more beautiful up close. Her skin was porcelain smooth and fragile, framed by jet black hair. A beauty mark at the right of her lower lip added to her mysterious air as she studied him, her lips lightly pursed.

"Leandra Gallagher." Her blue eyes were as cool and unreadable as aquamarine stones as she watched him, waiting almost expectantly.

For a moment he was taken aback. Was he supposed to know her or something? As he looked into the depths of her blue eyes, a picture flashed across the screen of his mind, but it flashed so quickly and the images were so blurred he couldn't be certain. Surely, he'd remember a face as distinctive as hers.

Well, if he didn't know her, why the hell was she looking at him like that? Then he remembered the rose in his hand and assumed she was waiting for him to give it to her. He held it out and, with a lazy grin, said, "I think this is for you."

"Thank you."

Her voice was low and sexy as hell, and her fingers brushed his as she took the rose from him. Todd watched her lift the flower's velvet petals to her nose and inhale deeply before dropping the long-stemmed rose beside her purse.

The husky voice, the blatant sexuality exuded in a gesture as simple as that of smelling a rose made Todd reevaluate the situation. He leaned a hip against the stage and crossed his arms, his muscular build threatening the seams of his tux while he studied her. Maybe she wasn't solid ice. Maybe, just maybe, someone warm and inviting was imprisoned within the icy exterior, waiting for a man like himself to crack through the glacial layers and free the woman trapped inside.

"You paid a hell of a lot of money for me. Think I'm worth it?" he asked with a teasing smile.

"I don't know, Dr. Stillman. You tell me. *Are* you worth it?"

Todd arched one eyebrow at her as he slowly straightened and offered her his arm. "Why don't we wait and let you draw your own conclusions?"

She returned his smile, but her smile was cool, not quite reaching her eyes. After picking up her purse, the rose, and a mink jacket slung across the back of her chair, she stood, hesitating for a moment before she slipped her arm through his and allowed him to lead her across the ball-room and out the double doors to the hallway beyond.

Todd dipped his head to be heard over the noise of the crowd. "Have you ever been to Mexico?"

"No."

"You'll love it. It's a beautiful country." His comment was met with silence. Frustrated, he thought, *Now what*? It was difficult carrying on a one-sided conversation. He searched his mind for something else to say and remembered other trips to Mexico and things he'd done there.

"Have you ever been snorkeling?"

At her second clipped no, he wondered if the woman was always this uptight. After a few more attempts at conversation, he gave up, deciding Mexico was going to be one hell of a long trip.

Just before they reached the desk, she stopped him with a gentle touch to his forearm. "Perhaps you could take care of this for me," she suggested as she withdrew her arm from his and opened her purse. After searching a moment, she removed a check and handed it to him.

As their hands touched, he noticed how fragile and trembly her fingers felt in his—like a frightened bird. Frowning slightly, he lifted his gaze to hers. What he saw reflected in the aquamarine depths of her eyes stopped him cold. Tears brightened her eyes, but a hostility as distinctive as the scent of the red rose she clutched in her hand etched her face.

"Tell me, Robert Todd Stillman II," she asked in a voice laced with tempered steel, "how does it feel to be bought and paid for?" Jerking her hand from his, she whirled around and hurried away, tossing the mink across her shoulders as she headed for the exit.

"Hey, wait!" Todd called after her, but she didn't even slow down. He watched her disappear through the hotel's double doors. *What in the hell's wrong with her*? he wondered irritably. He dipped his head to look at the check in his hand. It was made out to Leandra Gallagher and signed by Robert Todd Stillman.

His mind recoiled at the name. He hadn't written this check. He didn't even know this woman! Lifting his head, he looked at the door she'd disappeared through, then back at the check. At closer inspection, he recognized the distinctive scrawl of his father's signature. His gaze sought the date. The check was almost eight years old. He flipped it over and found written on the back in a neat and feminine handwriting, "Leandra Gallagher, Pay to order of Ballet Oklahoma."

Was this some kind of joke? If it was, he failed to see the humor. He glanced again in the direction of the door, then back at the check. What did she mean *bought and paid for*? His confusion slowly faded, and a feeling of revulsion swept over him when he realized who and what the woman must be.

"Dr. Stillman?"

The canary's voice penetrated Todd's churning thoughts. Numb, he looked blankly at the woman behind the desk.

"Are you ready to settle up?" she asked.

He looked again at the check, then quickly slipped it into the pocket of his tuxedo slacks. "Yes. Yes, I am."

He crossed to the desk and pulled his own checkbook from the inside pocket of his jacket. With the same detachment he used daily in surgery, he blanked out his emotions and focused on the exact movements of his hand as he deftly wrote out the check for five thousand dollars and signed his name . . . Dr. Robert Todd Stillman II.

# TWO

Leandra pressed the back of her hand to her mouth as she sagged against the side of her car. *Oh heavens, what have I done?* She glanced over her shoulder and was relieved to see he hadn't followed her out of the hotel yet. *Please, oh, please let me get away before he decides to follow me*, she thought hysterically.

Her fingers shaking, she groped in the darkness for the door lock. At last the key slid into place, and she yanked the door open and slipped inside, slamming the lock down behind her.

How stupid and childish to think she could even the score with Todd Stillman. The man hadn't even remembered her!

She glanced in the rearview mirror at her shadowed reflection, touching still-shaking fingers to her flushed cheeks. Granted, she didn't look very much like the seventeen-year-old girl he'd known. But—thanks to him—life had forced her to grow up fast, sharpening her features and giving her a more mature look than most women her age.

Her shoulders slumped against the seat as it occurred to her that maybe she had expected too much of Todd Stillman—at least in this instance. Just because his face was burned into her memory didn't mean hers was in his. But she knew without a doubt that even if he hadn't been introduced on the stage, she would have recognized him. He'd changed his hairstyle somewhat—his sideburns were shorter and the cut of his hair more conservative—but he still looked virtually the same.

When he'd leaned down to hand her the rose, she'd noticed the faint scar angling from his forehead about an inch into his scalp and remembered the story he'd told her of attempting a back flip and hitting the diving board with his head.

Leandra dropped her forehead to her hands atop the steering wheel. What had possessed her to seek him out for revenge? Years ago she had accepted her fate and had forced herself to forget Todd Stillman and his part in changing her life's direction. She could only assume the shock of seeing his picture in the paper had driven her to such ridiculous measures. It had been one thing to look at his picture in the relative safety of her living room but quite another to meet him face to face. She sucked in a deep breath and slowly released it, trying to slow her racing heart.

Whoever said revenge was sweet was either lying or crazy. In seeking to avenge a past wrong, she feared she might have opened Pandora's box, exposing herself and her carefully guarded secrets to the world. What if she'd angered Todd with her vengeful tactics and he decided to get even himself. What if—

*Trey! Dear God*, she thought in dismay, clapping her hands to her mouth. *What if Todd tried to take Trey away from her!*

\*　　\*　　\*

The fears continued to haunt Leandra on and off throughout the following day, interfering with her work and her peace of mind. They continued to plague her as she stumbled through the back door of her home, balancing a grocery sack, dry cleaning, and her purse.

The shrill ring of the phone sliced across the silent kitchen.

"Mrs. Brumbelow?" Leandra called as she hurried toward the kitchen desk while she silently counted the phone's rings. *Where is everyone*? she wondered in frustration as she juggled everything to one arm and snatched up the phone.

"Hello." She pressed the receiver between her ear and shoulder as she scooted the sack of groceries onto the kitchen counter.

"May I speak with Ms. Gallagher, please?"

Leandra frowned at the unfamiliar voice. If this was one of those telephone surveys, she was hanging up. "This is she."

"Hi, I'm Mrs. Roulf, Dr. Stillman's receptionist."

Leandra's purse slipped from her fingers and thudded against the floor, her body threatening to follow as she sank weakly onto the desk chair. She clutched the dry cleaning to her waist, wrinkling it into a wadded ball.

"Yes," she prompted in a shaky voice.

"Dr. Stillman asked me to call and offer his regrets. Due to his busy surgery schedule, he will be unable to accompany you on the trip to Ixtapa."

"I see." She really didn't *see* anything but was at a loss to say anything else.

"Please understand that Dr. Stillman fully intends to uphold his obligation and will pick up the tab for you and a guest of your choosing to take advantage of the trip."

Leandra was speechless.

"Ms. Gallagher?"

"Yes. Yes, I'm sorry, I'm still here." Her mind raced to think of a response. "Please thank Dr. Stillman for his generosity, but tell him I'm unable to accept his offer."

"Are you sure, Ms. Gallagher? After all, I understand you paid an awfully high price for the privilege of going."

"Yes, almost too high," Leandra whispered under her breath.

"I'm sorry, dear. I couldn't hear you."

"I said it was for a good cause."

"Yes, it was. The Stillmans have always taken great pride in their contributions to the charities," the receptionist proudly added.

Leandra's fingers tightened on the receiver as a picture of a young, innocent girl standing in the Stillman Corporation's plush offices while the senior Stillman wrote out a check flashed through her mind.

"Yes, they have, haven't they?" she said with a weary sigh. "Thank you for calling, Mrs. Roulf."

Leandra replaced the receiver and dropped her hands to her lap, pressing her palms together as she bowed her head. A huge weight lifted from her shoulders. "Thank you, thank you, thank you!" she whispered gratefully. She stood and draped the dry cleaning bag over the back of the chair before she turned to put away the groceries.

All day at the office she had worried about the repercussions of her rash actions of the night before, wondering what Todd Stillman had done with the check and wishing she'd never even read about the Bachelor Auction. Now it appeared her worries had been for naught.

Mentally replaying her conversation with Mrs. Roulf, she opened the refrigerator and shoved in a gallon of milk. *Busy surgery schedule indeed*! she recalled with a laugh.

Any other time, Leandra might have been upset at having been so obviously snubbed, but all she felt at the moment was an immense relief. It seemed her worries were over. She whistled a popular tune as she pushed the refrigerator door closed with a bump from her hip and headed for the rear stairway.

This time, she'd leave Todd Stillman in the past where he belonged!

The swinging doors from the surgery suite to the scrub room opened and Todd stepped through, peeling blood-stained gloves from his hands. He untied the top strings of his surgical mask and let it drop to his chest as he glanced back through the window to the digital wall clock in the operating room. If he'd hurry, he'd make it to his sister's house for dinner. He lifted one foot and hopped a few quick steps as he struggled to pull off one green paper shoe cover, then switched his weight to rip off the other.

After tossing them into the waste receptacle, he shrugged out of his surgical gown and stopped long enough to scrub his hands again before heading for the dressing room. Another glance at the clock and he decided to wear the green scrub suit to Ellen's instead of taking the time to change into his street clothes.

The family of the man he'd just operated on for the last four hours would be anxiously assembled in the waiting room. Good news for them. A quadruple bypass had been successfully completed and that, coupled with a change of life-style, would extend the man's life by several years. Todd would reassure the family, then run by the recovery room and check on his patient before he left the hospital.

After talking to the man's family, Todd slipped into the doctors' lounge to call his office.

"I won't be coming back to the office today," he informed his receptionist. "If you need me, I'll be at Ellen's house."

"Enjoy your evening, Dr. Stillman."

"Oh, wait! I almost forgot. Did you get in touch with Ms. Gallagher?"

"Yes, Doctor. She said to thank you for your generosity, but she couldn't accept your offer."

"What?" Todd didn't even attempt to disguise the surprise in his voice.

"That's what she said. I told her she'd paid a high enough price so she ought to take advantage, but she refused."

"Oh well, thanks for taking care of it for me."

"No problem. See you in the morning, Doctor."

Todd dropped the telephone receiver back onto its cradle, his forehead plowed into furrows of confusion. Now why in the world had she refused the trip? Granted, she hadn't really paid for it. He had. But if her purpose in purchasing him hadn't been to receive the trip, then why had she bought him?

With a shake of his head, he headed for the recovery room. Forget it, he told himself. At least he was free of her, and that's what he'd wanted when he'd instructed his receptionist to call her with his offer.

Winding up his responsibilities at the hospital took almost an hour, and Todd reached Ellen's just as his brother-in-law Wesley took the steaks off the grill. With his nose held high, Todd pushed through the wrought-iron gate opening onto the patio by the pool, sniffing the air as he made his way to the grill.

"Smells good. Enough for a hungry doctor?"

"Todd!" Wesley Jansen slapped his brother-in-law on the back in an affectionate greeting. "Always enough for you. Just getting through surgery?" he asked as he eyed Todd's green scrub suit.

Todd raked his fingers through his hair. "Yeah. Long day. The last case was a tough one, but the patient was doing fine when I left him in recovery."

"Hey, little brother!" Ellen swept out of the house, a heavy tray balanced in her hands. "Are you begging again?"

Todd laughed and tossed his wallet onto the patio table before taking the tray from his sister. "Always."

"I refuse to eat with a man dressed in putrid green. Go look in the closet in the utility room. I found a pair of your jeans in the dirty-clothes hamper the other day and washed them for you." She narrowed her eyes suspiciously at him. "Is that how you get your laundry done? Leaving a little bit here and there, hoping none of us will notice we're doing your laundry for you?"

"Gee. You caught me."

"Long ago, little brother, long ago. Oh, and there's probably a sweatshirt or something in there, too, so grab whatever. But hurry, dinner's ready."

Todd disappeared into the house, returning minutes later dressed in a pair of faded jeans and a sweatshirt that had almost as many holes as it did fabric.

Ellen passed him the salad bowl as he swung a leg over the back of a chair and sat down beside her. "Where are the kids?" he asked.

"Robby's at a ball game, and Prissy's spending the night with a friend. Blessed, isn't it?" Ellen said with a dramatic sigh.

Todd frowned. "What's blessed?"

"The silence! Didn't you notice?"

"To be honest, I kind of miss the noise. Silence I can get at my house."

After passing the salad bowl to Wesley, Todd loaded his plate with a large T-bone steak and a generous supply of French bread. Breakfast had consisted of a cup of coffee and a stale cinnamon roll, and lunch, a soft drink and candy bar gulped down in the doctors' lounge between surgery cases. He chuckled to himself as he thought of all the lectures on proper diet he'd delivered to his patients. If they knew what his own diet consisted of, they'd hang him from the flagpole in front of Mercy Hospital.

He tackled his steak while Ellen and Wes carried on an animated conversation. Todd listened but added little. Muscles tensed from hours spent in surgery slowly began to unwind. It felt good just to be outside after being confined within the walls of the hospital for over twelve hours.

He could almost taste the crisp tartness of autumn as he breathed deeply of the cool night air. This was his favorite time of year, a winding down of summer, a pensive time of reflection, as well as one of preparation. Since the age of five, the coming of autumn had always symbolized the beginning of another school term. New challenges to be met. Old hurts to escape.

But not this year. Oh, there would be challenges all right. A practice to establish. Patients to see. But no more school . . . no more running from a past he couldn't escape.

Taking a sip of iced tea, he glanced at his sister and wondered again how she managed to do it. She'd grown up in the same house he had. Shared the same parents and genes . . . the same secrets. Yet, she'd married and seemed happy enough.

Every time he stepped into Ellen's home he felt a sense of family and oneness. Something that had been absent in their childhood home. It almost made him want to try it for himself. Almost. Marriage wasn't for him. No way. He'd seen what love could do to a person, and he wasn't willing to take the gamble. Of course, it didn't keep every busybody he knew from trying to pair him off with someone. He frowned at his sister. The Bachelor Auction, he was sure, was just another ploy of hers to introduce him to some eligible female.

As if she'd read his thoughts, Ellen turned to him. "Who was the lady who bought you last night, Todd?"

His frown deepened, and he took a last bite of steak before answering. "Leandra Gallagher. Know her?"

Ellen's brow wrinkled as she thought for a moment. "No. The name's familiar, but I can't recall having met her." She turned to her husband. "Do you know her, Wes?"

"Gallagher." He frowned a moment, then shook his head. "Does sound familiar though."

Ellen pushed her plate away and relaxed in her chair. "Well, tell us about her."

Todd snorted. "The woman is a living and breathing iceberg. Five minutes with her was enough for me. I had my receptionist call her today and tell her I couldn't make the trip."

Ellen grabbed the arms of her chair and jerked herself forward. "You *what*?"

"Don't worry, sis. I offered to send her and a friend instead. Obviously, she wasn't too anxious to go either. She told Mrs. Roulf thanks but no thanks."

"Uh-oh."

Todd eyed his sister suspiciously. "Uh-oh, what?"

Ellen smiled weakly. "Well, I heard today that Butch and Ben McCain have agreed to do a special segment on their television show spotlighting the bachelor who raised the most money for Ballet Oklahoma."

"So? What does that have to do with me?"

"Five thousand dollars was the highest bid."

Todd's fork dropped from his fingers and clattered against his plate. "Oh, hell. You've got to be kidding."

Ellen winced. "No. The next highest bid was three thousand."

"But what about the candy man?"

"Who?"

"The candy man. The guy throwing out Hershey's Kisses."

Ellen laughed. "Oh, him. He only brought fifteen hundred."

Todd looked at her in surprise. "When I left, bids were flying back and forth across the room."

"Yes, well, he definitely stirred everything up. Unfortunately, the bids were low ones. But wasn't he cute and what a clever idea to throw—"

"Don't change the subject, Ellen. What about this Butch and Ben thing?"

Ellen sank back into her chair with a resigned sigh. "They plan to have you and your date on the show prior to your trip."

Todd dropped his forehead to his hands and raked his fingers through his hair, then lifted his head to glare at his sister. "This is all your fault, you know. For talking me into this damn thing in the first place and for arranging such a tempting trip. Why Mexico? And for Pete's sake, why four days and three nights in Mexico? Couldn't you have just offered a nice quiet dinner at the Greystone or something? Geez, sis."

Wesley Jansen chuckled as he watched the play between his wife and her little brother. It was good to see the two of them together again. Ellen had missed Todd while he'd been in medical school, and when he'd decided to remain at Duke University to specialize in cardiovascular thoracic surgery, she'd moped around the house for weeks. Ellen had been sure Todd was avoiding coming home, choosing to specialize as a means of delaying the inevitable confrontation. In Wesley's mind, he suspected she was right.

And it appeared Todd was still avoiding it. Only this morning Ellen had received a telephone call from her father, demanding to know why Todd had moved back to Oklahoma City and why he hadn't been informed of his son's plans. *Well,* Wesley thought, as a long sigh escaped him, *that's their problem, not mine. Todd and his father will have to work it out. I only hope Ellen doesn't get pulled into the line of fire.*

Todd threw down his napkin. "Well, I'm not going."

"You have to," Ellen cried. "Leandra Gallagher bought and paid for you."

"Damn it! Those were almost her same exact words!" Todd's chair grated against the brick patio as he pushed out of it and paced across the patio to the pool, shoving his hands deep into the back pockets of the faded jeans. After filling his lungs with several drafts of cool night air, he wheeled and stalked back to the table. "Look, Sis, I can assure you, the woman doesn't want to go to Mexico with me any more than I want to go with her. Whatever she hoped to gain from the situation, I can only assume she gained last night."

"Gained what? Todd, you're talking in riddles. Wesley," Ellen turned to her husband, "can you make any sense out of what he's saying?"

"No, dear. I can't. Perhaps Todd will enlighten us." Wesley studied the angry expression on his brother-in-law's face as Todd swung his leg back over the chair and sat down, resting his forearms against the wrought-iron patio table.

Todd spun his tea glass between his hands, watching the amber liquid swirl around its sides. His thoughts swirled with the same chaotic churning as he recalled the ice queen's beautiful face and those unforgettable eyes. "I only wish I could enlighten you."

Reaching for his wallet, he withdrew the check and dropped it on the table beside his brother-in-law's hand. As Wesley picked it up, Todd explained, "This is what she gave me last night to pay for her date."

Wesley passed the check to Ellen, whose eyes widened in surprise as she saw the signature. "But Daddy wrote this check!"

"I know. Look at the date."

"It's almost eight years old! Why would Daddy give her a check?"

With a snort of derision, Todd glanced at his sister. "You mean you can't figure it out? Hell, Ellen, Leandra Gallagher was one of Daddy's little playthings."

Ellen's jaw dropped open as she returned her gaze to the check clutched in her fingers. "But she's so young! Why, she couldn't have been more than twenty when this was written."

Todd took the check from Ellen and slipped it back into his wallet. "Probably some teenager fresh out of high school working in the steno pool at Dad's office."

"But why would he give her money?"

"That was his pattern. Play with them awhile, then when he became bored, he'd give them a little something to get rid of them."

"Oh, Todd! How could he do that to the poor girl?"

"*Poor girl*? That *poor girl* was a money-grabbing, husband-stealing minx! How can you feel sorry for her? Your sympathies would be better spent on Mother."

Silence hung heavy for a moment as the three sat at the

table staring at their empty plates. Wesley finally broke the silence.

"If that's the case, then why didn't she cash the check?"

No one could answer Wesley's question, least of all Todd. But it drew a series of suppositions. As they loaded the tray with the remains of their dinner and sought the warmth of indoors, they gathered and assimilated facts. Leandra Gallagher had bought a weekend date with Todd Stillman with an outdated check written by Todd's father and paid to her. From this they established two possible motivations. She was a gold digger looking for a free trip and had used the check like blackmail, knowing Todd would never want the check to go public. Or perhaps she had an ax to grind with their father and had chosen to use Todd to get even with him.

But each theory brought them full circle. If it was money she wanted, why hadn't Leandra Gallagher simply cashed the check years ago?

Realizing their theories weren't solving their problem, they then discussed how best to handle the situation.

The McCain brothers complicated matters. Their offer to further publicize the charity event was a boon for Ballet Oklahoma and its need to raise money—one every person on the committee would be anxious to take advantage of. To make matters worse, everyone who'd attended the auction knew which bachelor brought the highest bid, so it would be foolish to assume someone other than Todd could appear on the show.

The three finally agreed that Todd would have to appear with Leandra Gallagher on the show to avoid awkward explanations.

"But that's as far as my responsibility goes, Ellen," Todd warned his sister. "I refuse to take that woman to

Mexico. And I won't make the arrangements for the television show. You'll have to take care of all the details. After all, you're the one who got us into this mess."

No one regretted *this mess*, as Todd insisted on referring to the situation, any more than Ellen.

Since she had served as co-chair for the auction, it wasn't difficult for her to secure Leandra Gallagher's telephone number and address from the list of registered participants of the auction. The following afternoon, as she dialed Leandra's home number, her hand trembled. How did one go about talking to her father's former mistress? Ellen suppressed a hysterical giggle as she pressed her palm to her forehead. This was incredible!

At the pert hello from the other end of the line, Ellen's fingers tightened on the receiver. There was no escaping the confrontation now. "Leandra?"

"No, this is Mrs. Brumbelow, her housekeeper. Leandra's still at the office. Would you like to leave a message?"

*Housekeeper*! She suppressed a laugh. If Todd was right, Leandra Gallagher had certainly climbed from the ranks of the steno pool. "No. I really need to talk with her now. Would it be possible for me to call her at work?"

"I'm sure she wouldn't mind. Her number is 555-7669, extension 36."

After jotting down the number, Ellen replaced the receiver and sank back against her chair. Her curiosity piqued, she retrieved the phone and, using the eraser end of her pencil, punched in Leandra's office number.

"Leandra Gallagher, please."

"This is Leandra."

"Hi, Leandra. I'm Ellen Jansen, co-chair of the Bachelor Auction."

"Yes?"

Ellen heard the hesitancy in Leandra's voice but ignored it. "Since you were the highest bidder at the Bachelor Auction, Butch and Ben McCain would like to have you and Todd appear on their show. I'm calling to arrange the details concerning the taping."

There was a slight pause before Leandra's cool voice replied. "I'm sorry, Ms. Jansen, but I'm afraid that's impossible. Thank you for calling."

Before Ellen had a chance to explain, there was a click and the dial tone hummed in her ear. Surprised, she stared at the receiver a moment before replacing it. Todd was right, she decided. The woman was one cold fish.

*Now what?* Ellen wondered as she pushed back her chair. She tapped her pencil against her cheek as she tried to think of an alternate plan. But there wasn't one. The only option remaining was to call Todd and tell him she'd failed.

With a sigh of defeat, she picked up the phone again and punched in Todd's office number. "Mrs. Roulf? Ellen. Is Todd in surgery this afternoon?"

"No. As a matter of fact, he's in his office dictating. Would you like to speak with him?"

"Yes, please."

A moment later Todd's voice came across the line. "Did you arrange everything?"

"No." Ellen winced at the angry oath that followed her denial. "I tried. She refused to do the show and hung up on me before I could explain anything. Maybe you should talk to her."

"Me! *You* were supposed to make the arrangements. All *I* was supposed to do was show up for the taping!"

"I know. And I tried. I really did. But she hung up before I had a chance to discuss it. Now what'll we do?"

Ellen heard the note of angry frustration in her brother's voice when he snapped, "Never mind. I'll take care of it."

One option Todd hadn't considered occurred to him while he finished up his afternoon rounds at Mercy Hospital. It was so simple and so obvious he was amazed he hadn't thought of it before. Call Butch McCain. He and Butch had known each other in college, and Todd hoped to take advantage of that friendship to weasel out of the mess.

In the doctors' lounge, he pulled his wallet from the back pocket of his slacks before he sat down on the couch and dragged the phone from the end table to his lap. Cradling the receiver between his ear and shoulder, he flipped open the phone book and found Butch McCain's number. After punching it in, he waited, nervously strumming his fingers against the pages of the telephone book.

"Hello."

"Butch? Todd Stillman."

"Todd! Hey, man, it's been a while."

Todd laughed. "Yeah, it has. How've you been?"

"Good. Good. And you?"

"Can't complain." Todd cleared his throat. "Listen, Butch, about this bachelor thing—"

"Ben and I couldn't believe it when we heard it was you who brought the five grand. Is the lady blind or what?"

Todd held the receiver at arm's length for a moment while Butch's roar of laughter crossed the phone wires, then brought the receiver back to his ear. "Are you kidding? I was thinking she hadn't paid quite enough."

Butch laughed again.

"Listen, Butch, the lady and I are having a hard time

getting together. With my surgery schedule and all, it's pretty tough. We want to thank you for the offer of having us on your show, but it looks like we won't be able to arrange it.''

''No problem, buddy. You and the little lady just pick out a time that suits you, and we'll tape at your convenience. I can have a camera crew ready when you are.''

All hope of escaping the fiasco seeped out of Todd. ''Thanks, Butch,'' he said, having to dig deep for the proper enthusiasm. ''I appreciate it. I'll be back in touch.''

Pressing his thumb against the button to break the connection, Todd dropped his head against the back of the sofa. Only one thing left to do. He picked up his wallet and slipped a piece of paper from it. Releasing the button, he punched in the number scrawled there.

''Hello,'' a feminine voice answered.

''Leandra?''

''Yes?''

''Todd Stillman. It seems we have a problem. The McCain brothers want us to appear on their show.''

''I've already discussed this with a Ms. Jansen and explained to her that it's impossible for me to do this.''

''I know. And I called Butch McCain to decline, but now he's offered to have a crew at our disposal to conform to our schedules.''

''I'm sorry, Dr. Stillman, you'll just have to do it alone.''

Click, then dial tone.

Todd angrily punched in the number again but received a busy signal.

''Damn that woman!'' He slammed the receiver down and shoved the phone back to the end table. He stood and jammed his wallet into his back pocket.

Snatching the piece of paper with Leandra's phone number and address from the sofa seat, he wheeled around and stormed out of the doctors' lounge, muttering under his breath, "You got us into this mess, lady, and, by God, you'll help me get us out!"

Midway up the freestanding staircase, Leandra paused, halted by the musical chimes of the front doorbell. She leaned over the banister and called in the direction of the kitchen, "I'll get it, Mrs. Brumbelow!"

Hurrying back down the stairway, Leandra reached the front door just as the chimes pealed a second time. When she pulled open the heavy oak door, she found Todd Stillman standing with both arms braced high against the door frame. Obviously sensing her intent, he quickly stuck one foot in the doorway to prevent her from slamming the door in his face.

"I said we have a problem, and since *you* are the cause of the problem, *you* are going to help figure a way out of this mess whether you like it or not!"

Leandra glanced nervously over her shoulder before brushing past Todd and pulling the door to behind her. "I told you, I can't do it."

Todd leaned back against the two-story wood column fronting the house, his gaze narrowed at her. "So you say. Unfortunately, it's already been announced on television that the bachelor drawing the largest bid—as well as the woman making the bid—will make a guest appearance on *The McCain Brothers' Show*. Since everyone at the auction knows your five thousand dollar bid was the highest, they'll expect to see you and me."

"There has to be another solution."

Todd shrugged. "I'm listening."

"Surely . . ." Leandra's voice drifted off as she realized the futility of the situation.

"I hope you understand the magnitude of the predicament you've placed us all in."

Catching her lower lip between her teeth, Leandra bowed her head while color warmed her face. She knew only too well—more so than he did. When she'd gone to the auction, she'd assumed only the two of them would be involved. She'd hand him the check, satisfy her need for revenge, and then disappear, just as he'd disappeared years before. But now things were snowballing out of control. To avoid the taping, Leandra knew explanations would be necessary, and she didn't want anyone, least of all Todd, delving into her reasons for avoiding him and this public display.

Knowing the safest path was to cooperate, she lifted her eyes to Todd's and met his steely gaze. "I'm sorry. Truly, I am. I—I'll do whatever is necessary to end this nightmare."

"Good." Todd pushed off the column. "Be at the television station at 5:30 Monday morning unless you hear otherwise from me. We tape at 6:30."

He went down two steps, then turned. "Oh, and by the way, don't think this means I'm taking you to Ixtapa, because I'm not." With that, he turned on his heel and strode to the low-slung Jaguar parked in the driveway.

Leandra had to bite her tongue to keep from shouting back at him, *Don't worry, because I wouldn't go anyway*, but she dared not antagonize the man. It was best to cooperate and end the ordeal as quickly and painlessly as possible.

# THREE

The heat radiating from the bright camera lights drew a fine mist of perspiration across Todd's forehead. Beside him, Leandra looked cool and collected as usual. She had maintained that same cool facade throughout the taping. Carefully skirting the McCain brothers' probing questions, she had responded with answers that revealed nothing about herself or her private life.

Butch and Ben were smooth interviewers, and as the program progressed, Todd relaxed, knowing the two brothers were winding down to the end of the segment. Soon it would be over.

Butch straightened his bow tie. "Ben? What do you think about the two of us taking a little trip?"

Instantly, Todd tensed.

"Sounds good to me. Where did you have in mind?"

"How about Ixtapa, Mexico? We could sort of follow these two around and maybe do a show from there. What do you think, Jake? Want to go to Mexico?"

Camera one turned to focus on the man behind camera

two. His face hidden by the massive equipment in front of him, Jake gave Ben a thumbs-up signal, showing his consent.

Leandra's jaw sagged. "No," she whispered. Todd grabbed her hand and squeezed like a vise. Snapping her head around to look at him, she saw his silent warning.

"What do you think, Leandra?" Ben asked. "Would you mind if Butch and I tagged along on your date?"

Quickly, Leandra smoothed her features just as camera two zoomed in for a close-up of her face. It was difficult since she felt as if her insides were being ripped apart. The decision to go to Mexico was no longer simply hers or Todd's to make. Once this show aired, the entire city would know about the trip and would be waiting to watch the next segment, the trip to Mexico itself. What could she possibly say to Ben's request? *No, I'm sorry. You see, I didn't really want to go to Mexico with Todd. I just wanted to hurt him like he'd hurt me eight years ago.*

But she couldn't say that. That would only raise more questions, questions she didn't want to answer. She was trapped by her own vengeful act.

Realizing this, she smiled and forced a note of enthusiasm into her voice as she replied, "No, I don't mind." She glanced at Todd, and her stomach did a backward flip. Though she was sure no one else noticed, she was aware of the tension in the set of his jaw. He didn't want to go to Mexico any more than she did.

Her next thought was just as distressing. How would she ever explain all this to John and Trey?

The only consolation was that she and Todd wouldn't be alone. With that thought in mind, she turned back to Butch and added with a carefree shrug, "The more the merrier."

*       *       *

Due to Todd's surgery schedule, the flight he'd chosen for Mexico had been a late one, and they arrived at their destination after dark. Fortunately, Butch and Ben McCain had chosen the same flight. From their seats across the aisle, they had carried on a running dialogue with Todd, sparing Leandra the task of making small talk with her date. To the McCain brothers this trip was a lark.

To Leandra Gallagher it was a nightmare.

The countryside they traveled through to reach their hotel was hilly and covered with a wild undergrowth of knotty vegetation. Butted against the hills were small huts. Through their open doors Leandra could see Mexican families busy at their nightly tasks, spotlighted in their activities by a lone electric bulb swinging from the ceiling.

The night air blowing through the open taxi window was cool against Leandra's cheeks. Worry over the forced proximity promised by the weekend with Todd Stillman left her feeling feverish and weak.

Upon their arrival at the Camino Real Hotel, her worries partially dissipated when the bellhop opened the door to their suite and revealed two separate bedrooms, confirming Todd's promise that they wouldn't be sharing a room.

The floor of the sitting room adjoining the two bedrooms, as well as the remainder of the suite, was covered with a rust-colored Mexican tile. Deep cushioned sofas were angled to take advantage of the breathtaking view of the jagged cliffs and the ocean that lay beyond the open sliding doors.

The roar of the surf and the smell of its salty spray drew Leandra out onto the patio and into the cool night air, leaving Todd alone to deal with the bellboy.

A hammock hung from heavy beams on her right. Pots of red and pink bougainvillaeas surrounded a small private pool on her left. Any other time she would have gloried in so much color and splendor. But not tonight. Every nerve ending in her body stretched taut in awareness of the man in the room behind her whose footsteps she heard moving toward her.

"Pretty, isn't it?"

"Yes, it is." Leandra continued to stand with her back to Todd, her gaze riveted on the waves exploding against the rocks below.

He stopped beside her and leaned out over the ledge, the heat of his body warm against her bare arm. Automatically, she stepped away.

Her action didn't go unnoticed by Todd. Frowning, he turned to face her, resting his hip against the balcony's stucco ledge while crossing his arms across his chest. "I'm not going to bite you."

Leandra snapped her head around to look at him, then quickly glanced away again. "I know."

"Then why do you jump every time I get within two feet of you?"

"I don't," she replied defensively.

"Yes, you do. You—oh, never mind." He dropped wearily onto one of the lounge chairs on the patio and stretched out, locking his fingers behind his head. "If we're going to pull this off, we need to set some ground rules. I don't particularly care how you feel about me or about being in Mexico, but whenever Butch and Ben McCain are around, you are going to act like you're having the time of your life.

"First thing in the morning, we're going deep-sea fishing and, after that, snorkeling on Ixtapa Island. We'll have lunch in a café on the island, and I expect you to cooperate. You'll act like you would with any other man you might be with on a date. And that means not jumping every time I get near you."

"Will the McCains be with us?"

"Probably."

Relief flooded Leandra. With the McCain brothers there, she wouldn't be alone with Todd. "Don't worry. I'll play my part."

Todd watched her fingers relax on the ledge's rough surface. Anger bubbled up in him. All during the flight to Mexico, she'd kept her nose buried in a book, and on the taxi ride to the hotel she'd hugged the car door and watched the scenery, though God only knew what she thought she could see in the pitch darkness. And all to avoid him.

"If you're so worried about being alone with me, why did you want this *date*?"

She lifted a shoulder and let it drop. "I don't know. At the time, it seemed like the thing to do."

"And what's that supposed to mean?"

"It was a mistake. That's all."

"Yes, and an expensive one I had to pay for."

Leandra dipped her head when reminded of the expenses he'd borne. She'd known when she'd given Todd the check that he couldn't give it to Ballet Oklahoma. Her intent had been to hurt him, as she had been hurt eight years before. Unfortunately, she had never carried her vengeful plan beyond the moment she handed him the check.

"I'm sorry," she murmured, then raised her head to stare at the jagged cliffs beyond. "I'll pay you back. It'll take awhile, but I promise you'll get your money."

"Forget it. It's a tax write-off anyway. But you still haven't answered my question. Why did you bid on me? Was it to get the trip?"

"No."

"Then why?"

*Why? Why? Why?* The word slammed against Leandra with the same jarring intensity as that of the ocean's waves crashing against the rocks below, eating away at her self-control. Goaded by the unrelenting questions, Leandra whirled around, her eyes sparking dangerously. "Revenge. I wanted revenge."

"Revenge on my father?"

Realizing she'd said more than she should, Leandra brushed past Todd and headed for the sliding glass door. "I'm tired. I'm going inside."

He lunged and caught her by the arm before she could slip past him. He'd figured out the relationship between his father and Leandra when he'd first seen the check, but he wanted to hear it from her. "Why did he give you the check?" he demanded, his fingers tightening on the soft skin of her forearm.

She winced. "You're hurting me."

His grip loosened, but he didn't release her. Sensing he would accept no more evasion, Leandra turned her head until she met his steely gaze with one of defiance. "He gave me the check to get rid of me. To buy me off. *Now* are you satisfied?"

Light streaming through the open doorway turned the tears building in Leandra's eyes to glimmering diamonds. The tears told him more than her words. His father had hurt her. And Todd knew about hurt. His fingers slackened on her arm, and she wrenched free and ran to her room, slamming the door behind her. He heard the soft click of the lock that followed, and that only irritated him more.

Locking the door wasn't necessary. Unlike his father, Todd Stillman never forced his affections on any woman. He dropped his head back against the padded cushion on the lounge chair. But Leandra didn't know that. She probably figured he was just like his father. Out to get his pleasure without regard for the other person's feelings or needs.

Ever since he'd learned as a teenager of his father's philandering ways, Todd had borne a deep resentment for the man. The feeling had festered until that awful day he had come home unexpectedly and found his mother sitting in the kitchen staring blankly at the wall . . . and his father in the guest bedroom with another woman. On that day the resentment had blossomed into a full-blown hate.

"Damn you, Dad," he muttered to the dark star-studded night. "How many lives have you ruined with your tom-catting ways?"

Sand clung to Leandra's legs and arms, but she ignored it, along with the fly that buzzed at her ear. Stretched out on a beach towel, her hat brim pulled low on her brow, she closed her eyes against the glare of the midday sun and allowed her body to relax.

Ben and Jake were out skiing, and Butch and Todd were in the open-air café where she'd left them, talking football. Without them, she felt a sense of relief. No cameras to smile for. No part for her to play.

Though she was reluctant to admit it, Todd Stillman was getting under her skin. His questions the night before concerning her relationship with his father still nagged at her. After eight years of avoiding people's prying questions, Leandra was adroit in the art of evasion and hoped she had led Todd to make the wrong assumption.

And that's what bothered her. Even though she knew it was necessary, she hadn't wanted Todd to think she'd had an affair with his father. But it couldn't be helped, she thought with a sigh. The alternative would certainly have been worse.

Children played at the edge of the water, their laughter

wafting to Leandra as they built sand castles and dug for shells. She listened to their excited voices and thought wistfully of Trey. He'd love Mexico, she was sure, though he'd never be satisfied to sunbathe on the beach. He would insist on participating in every activity available—snorkeling, parasailing, deep-sea fishing. So much like his father.

Leandra frowned at the thought, yet she couldn't deny it. Trey was like his father.

"Mind if I join you?"

Leandra lifted the brim of her hat to find Todd looking down at her. "No." Reluctantly, she sat up, scooting to one end of the colorful beach towel to make room for him. So much for privacy.

He picked up her bottle of sunscreen and sat down. "You mind?" he asked, holding the bottle up for her approval.

"No. Help yourself."

From the corner of her eye she watched him squirt lotion onto his palm, then rub it up and down his arms and across his chest. He strained to spread some across his shoulders and back.

"Here, I'll do that." She took the bottle and immediately regretted the impulsive offer when he turned his back to her, his shoulders rolled forward, his wrists draped over his knees. Tanned skin stretched over well-honed muscles, but it was the narrow trail of his spine that held her spellbound. From the nape of his neck her gaze traveled down each vertebra to the elasticized waist of his jams. She sucked in a long breath.

Todd cocked his head over his shoulder. "Problem?"

"Uh . . . no." Hurriedly, Leandra squirted the white sunscreen in a wild arc across his back. He flinched when the cold lotion hit his skin.

He frowned over his shoulder at her. "You could have warmed it with your hands first."

Biting back a smile, she said, "Sorry." She smoothed the cream across his back, working her hands from his shoulders down the agonizingly long length of his spine, then back up. She tried to blot out the softness of his skin and the strength she sensed beneath her fingertips but failed. Of their own accord, her fingers played down the length of spine, dipping and rising over each swell.

Todd closed his eyes and dropped his chin to his chest. A moan of pleasure escaped him as her fingers gently kneaded, melting away the tension in his muscles. "I could sure use you after a day in surgery. Your fingers are magic."

Immediately, Leandra dropped her hands to her sides, shocked by their traitorous actions. "I think you're covered now."

The slight breathlessness in her voice as she drew away from him made Todd realize she, too, had been affected by the brief contact. Unlike for him, the intimacy seemed to make her even more uncomfortable with him, something he had hoped to alleviate by joining her on the beach. Determined to put her at ease, he leaned back on his elbows and looked out over the water. "Beautiful, isn't it?"

With her gaze fixed on the sea, she replied, "Yes, it is."

They sat in silence and watched the waves roll closer and closer on the beach, sending the children running while destroying the sand castle they had made. It was a comfortable silence, yet Todd resented it. He saw it as another ploy Leandra used to alienate herself from him. Maybe it was only because he loved a challenge, but he was determined to break down the barriers she erected between them. "Have you ever built a sand castle?"

"No. Have you?"

"A few." He glanced at her. "Want to build one?"

Leandra laughed softly. "I wouldn't know where to begin."

Todd caught her hand and pulled her reluctantly to her feet. "Come on. It's easy. I'll show you."

He picked up the bucket abandoned by the children and began scooping up sand. "We'll start with the main castle, then add from there." He dumped the sand, then handed the bucket to Leandra. While he smoothed the rounded shape, Leandra scooped up more sand.

The main building of the castle grew until it reached in towering layers to Leandra's knees. Engrossed in the project, she dropped the bucket and picked up a stick and began to etch windows into the hard-packed sand.

Intrigued by her deft movements, Todd sat back on his heels and watched. Wisps of dark hair had escaped the confines of her hat and blew across her face, drawing his gaze there. Her expression was intense yet animated as she worked to add dimension and depth to the sand.

All signs of the ice queen were gone, leaving a woman warm and vibrant and very much alive. Throughout the day, he'd caught glimpses of this side of Leandra, but only when Butch and Ben were present—never when they were alone. Whenever it was just the two of them, she seemed to withdraw into herself, presenting that same damn cool facade.

Oblivious to his perusal, Leandra caught her bottom lip between her teeth as she crawled around the castle, adding here, smoothing there. From the sand beside her knee, she pulled a rusty bottle cap and filled it, carefully emptying it at selected spots to further embellish the castle.

"Are you an artist?"

She glanced up at him, then laughed as she dribbled a combination of sand and water over the edge of the castle wall, creating battlements. "No. But I've had a lot of experience with mud pies. My sisters and I used to make the most intricate cakes and confections out of mud."

"To eat?"

She laughed again. "No, but once we talked our little brother Jimmy into eating one. We told him it was chocolate." She sat back and cocked her head, studying their creation. "It needs something." She glanced at Todd. "What's missing?"

"Turrets. Every castle needs turrets." He scooped a handful of sand and quickly shaped a tower at each corner. "And a moat." He cupped his fingers and dragged them around the perimeters of the castle.

While Todd scooped out sand, Leandra filled the bucket with water from the ocean. She poured it into the moat, watching it fill the narrow recess. Kneeling at the side of the castle, she threaded a strand of hair behind her ear. "There. Now it's perfect."

Drawn by the movement of her graceful fingers, Todd focused on her profile. Thick dark lashes framed almond-shaped eyes and brushed against a slash of high cheekbones as she squinted up at the bright sun. His gaze riveted on her, he answered in a suddenly husky voice, "Yes. Perfect."

Leandra lowered her gaze to the castle, unaware of Todd's scrutiny. "And who do you suppose lives in this perfect castle?"

"Some bloodthirsty king."

Leandra frowned as she formed a drawbridge out of sticks. "Powerful, but not bloodthirsty. And his queen. Every king must have a queen."

"Why?"

"Continuation of the line, you know."

"Poor woman. Probably kidnapped her from some un-suspecting laird and keeps her locked up in the tower until she promises to deliver him a son."

"Not this king. He may have kidnapped her, but he did so out of love, not for power or assurance of a successor."

Todd snorted. "You're a hopeless romantic."

Leandra raised her chin and glared at him indignantly. "And what are you?"

Todd's mouth twisted into a grim line. "A realist. Wise enough to know few people ever find happiness in love. I'd have thought my dad had taught you that much."

Before Leandra could reply, he reached out his hand and pulled her to her feet. "Here come Butch and Ben. I think they want some shots of us walking on the beach."

Wesley Jansen opened his office door and, with a look only a principal can effectively deliver, gave a last stern warning to the sullen fourth-grader before sending the boy back to his classroom. Just as he turned to close his door, a red-faced boy burst into the reception area.

"Come quick," the boy gasped. "A kid fell off the monkey bars."

Wesley grabbed a first-aid kit from under the counter and raced out the door. Accidents were a common occur-rence on elementary school playgrounds, but no matter the degree of injury, it was his policy to respond personally to each one. Reports must be filed, and he preferred to know firsthand what had happened.

When he arrived on the playground, he found the stu-dents huddled around the monkey bars. As he pushed his way through the mass of children, he sensed this was more than a scraped knee or a bloody lip. The stricken look on the face of the playground monitor and the limp body she knelt beside confirmed his suspicions.

Immediately, he took charge. He turned to a young wide-eyed boy, took him by the shoulder, and ordered, "Go to the office and tell Mrs. Simpson to call an ambulance."

With a last anxious look over his shoulder, the boy raced off as Wesley dropped to a knee beside the frazzled teacher. He put his fingers to the child's wrist and found a pulse, weak though it was. "What happened?"

"I don't know exactly." The teacher's voice broke, and she swallowed hard to gain control. "The children said he fell. He was unconscious when I got here." She pointed to a lump on the side of the child's head. "It looks like he hit his head when he fell, and his left arm doesn't look right. It just kind of . . . well, hangs."

Wesley gently ran a hand down the length of the boy's arm. He felt the unusual contortion and swelling of the bone.

His voice remained calm but firm. "Mrs. Wagner, I want you to go to the office and pull the boy's file. Call his parents and have them meet us at Mercy Hospital. Then call the doctor listed in case of emergency and have him meet us there, too."

Obviously relieved to have someone else in charge, Mrs. Wagner hurried to the office. After making the required calls, she returned to the playground just as the ambulance squealed to a stop at the side of the school.

After assessing the situation, the ambulance attendants strapped the boy to a board and gently leveled him onto the gurney.

"The boy's mother is out of the country. His grandmother and their pediatrician will be meeting you at the emergency room." Wesley listened to the teacher's hurried report as he helped guide the gurney into the waiting ambulance.

He climbed in beside the still semi-conscious boy and grasped the child's cool left hand in his, careful not to disturb the broken arm. The door slammed shut and Wesley struggled for balance as the ambulance took off, its siren squealing overhead.

A woman stood in the waiting room slowly knotting a handkerchief between shaking fingers.

"Are you Trey's grandmother?" Wesley asked. At her anxious nod, he moved to stand near her. "I'm Wesley Jansen, Trey's school principal. The boy is conscious now. As soon as the orthopedic surgeon finishes setting his arm, you can see him." Wesley noted the paleness of the woman's face and quickly guided her to a chair. "Could I get you a cup of coffee or something?"

"No. No, I'm fine." She smiled weakly. "I have nine children, and seven of them have suffered broken bones of one kind or another. Some of them more often than others." Her cheeks puffed slightly as she blew out a long breath of relief. "But I don't think I've ever been as frightened as I was when I received the call from the school telling me my grandson had been in an accident."

"I believe that comes with the territory of being a grandmother."

She chuckled, color slowly seeping back into her pale cheeks. "No. I attribute it to the fact his mother is in Mexico. If she were here, she would be doing the fainting and I, the fanning."

Thankful the woman was obviously not going to pass out on him, Wesley relaxed. His student was in the capable hands of one of Oklahoma City's finest orthopedic surgeons. Things were under control. "It never fails.

Nothing ever happens to a child until his parents are out of pocket.''

The woman stiffened slightly, and Wesley wondered what he'd said to cause her to withdraw perceptibly from him.

"Do you know my grandson, Mr. Jansen?"

"No, I'm sorry to say I don't. I've only been principal of this school for about six weeks. I haven't met all of my students or their parents."

"I see." She smoothed her dress over her knees, then turned and looked him square in the eye. "I'm Agnes *Gallagher*, Trey's maternal grandmother."

The emphasis she placed on her last name told Wesley all he needed to know. Since the child bore his mother's maiden name, he assumed there was no father in the picture.

"Trey has no . . ." Wesley couldn't bring himself to finish the sentence.

"No. He has no father."

"I'm sorry. I just . . ." Again he found himself without adequate words to express his remorse over his thoughtless referral to the child's parents.

"No need for an apology. We all accepted the circumstances of Trey's birth long ago." Mrs. Gallagher bent her head a moment, but when she lifted her face to look at Wesley again, there was a proud lift to her chin. "My daughter is a wonderful mother, Mr. Jansen. She's devoted to Trey and to his happiness, almost to the exclusion of her own." She shook her head and glanced away from Wesley's penetrating gaze. "It must be difficult being a single parent—being solely responsible for a child's welfare as well as his support. But she never complains and seldom asks for help.

"I guess that's why we were all so surprised when she

called to tell us she was taking this trip. She's never gone away alone before.'' A weary sigh escaped her. ''I really hate to call her and tell her about Trey's accident. She'll insist on coming home, and Leandra needs this time away.''

*Leandra*? The name hit him like a ton of bricks. Leandra Gallagher was the woman with his brother-in-law in Ixtapa. He'd never met Leandra. He was only familiar with the young woman as described by Todd and Ellen. He tried to associate the coldhearted gold digger Todd had sketched with the devoted, selfless mother the woman sitting with him had described, but the two descriptions just wouldn't jibe.

''Your daughter is Leandra Gallagher?''

''Yes. Why?''

Wesley shook his head in bewilderment. ''Todd Stillman is my brother-in-law.'' At the woman's puzzled look, Wesley added, ''The man your daughter is with in Mexico.

''Hey! Wait, you two.'' Ben's voice stopped Todd and Leandra in midstride in the open-air hallway of the Camino Real. ''Just look at that sunset.''

The two turned in unison to look over the bank of flowers bordering the hallway in the direction Ben pointed. The sun, in its descent, bled through the blue sky in smeared bands of purple, red, and gold. Transformed by the majestic display, Todd and Leandra stood side by side and stared.

Behind them, Ben's voice clipped orders to his film crew. ''Get your camera ready, Jake. Don't move, you two. This is perfect.''

Other than the whooshing of the waves rolling in as the

tide rushed out to sea, the soft whir of the camera was the only sound that could be heard.

Without realizing he'd done it, Todd slipped his fingers through Leandra's. "Perfect," Ben said in a stage whisper behind them. "Focus on the two of them, Jake, but make sure you have the sun banking between them. Now I want you two to slowly turn toward each other. Good. Good. Now . . ."

His voice drifted into nothingness as Todd's gaze met the aquamarine depths of Leandra's. All day they had played their parts as a young couple on a romantic vacation. At some point during the day their roles had become confused while they'd laughed and played before the ever-present camera, blending real emotions with their playacting, until Todd could no longer distinguish between what was reality and what was pretense.

After a day spent fishing on the open sea and snorkeling off the reefs of Ixtapa Island, the wind and surf had whipped Leandra's hair loose from the tight chignon she usually wore. Now, tendrils of her coal-black hair brushed her shoulders and feathered her face.

Todd reached up and twined a loose strand behind her ear. The camera was forgotten as were Butch and Ben McCain as Todd slipped his hand beneath the weight of her hair and cupped the back of her neck, drawing her to him. They became one with the sun and the passionate bands of color surrounding it their halo as their lips met for the first time.

His lips, his kiss, the taste of him were just as she remembered, and Leandra willingly accepted him as she had on that sweet summer night so many years before. For now, there was no past, no present—only the moment. And they seized it as one.

"Great! Are you getting this, Jake?" Ben turned to the

cameraman and caught Jake's affirmative thumbs-up signal. "This is perfect. Now fade to focus on the sunset beyond them . . . annnnnd cut. Good. That's a wrap."

Ben's voice at last penetrated Leandra's fogged mind, and she dragged her lips from Todd's and twisted away from him, her chest rising and falling as she grabbed deep gulps of the sea air. Below her, the sun's retreating rays glowed like a river of molten gold on the ocean's smooth surface. She felt as if that same phosphorus river had seeped within her, filling her with its warm, delicious radiance.

How could she have allowed him to kiss her like that and in front of the camera no less? "If you'll excuse me," she whispered in a choked voice and turned and fled to the suite, her face throbbing with the warmth of her embarrassment.

# FOUR

Minutes later, when Todd entered the suite, Leandra had already disappeared into her room.

"Leandra?" He paused, listening for her answer, but heard instead the sound of water running in her bathroom. Sighing in frustration, he flopped down on the sofa, dragging a weary hand through his hair. What had gotten into him? Why had he kissed her? The trip was complicated enough. He certainly didn't need to compound it.

Out of the corner of his eye, he saw the red light on the phone blinking, signaling a message. Years of responding to flashing red lights made him reach for the phone.

"This is Dr. Stillman in Suite 48. Do you have a message for me?" A frown cut across his brow as he quickly picked up a pen and paper from the end table and jotted down the number the desk clerk gave him.

In the bathroom, Leandra splashed water over her face to cool her flushed cheeks. The heat flaming there was the result of more than just too many hours in the sun. Todd

Stillman had put it there and a matching fire low in her abdomen—and with only one kiss. She covered her face with the cool wet cloth, hiding the passion-glazed eyes the mirror exposed.

A knock sounded on the bathroom door. She ignored it.

"Leandra? There's a message for you to call your mother."

Immediately, Leandra dropped the cloth as her thoughts flew to Trey. Something had happened, she was sure. It was the only reason her mother would call.

She jerked open the door. "What's wrong? What's happened?"

Surprised by her stricken expression, Todd tried to reassure her. "Nothing as far as I know. There's just a message for you to call your mother."

Leandra ran for the phone, grabbed it, and began to dial as she sank onto the sofa. Twice she was forced to start over because her fingers shook so hard. Finally, Todd took the phone from her and completed the call. When he heard the first ring, he passed her the phone, then sat down on the edge of the coffee table opposite her and waited.

"Mother? It's Leandra. What's wrong?"

Unable to hear the response from the other end, Todd could only conclude from the moisture building in Leandra's eyes as she listened to her mother's reply that something bad had indeed happened.

"Oh, no." Leandra bit down hard on her lower lip. "How—how is he?" She drew her hand into a tight fist on her lap. Todd picked it up and squeezed it reassuringly.

"Could I talk to him?" She turned her face away from Todd as a tear slipped from the corner of her eye and streamed unchecked down her face. Sensing her need for privacy, he released her hand and stood. As he walked away, he heard her say, "Trey? How are you, darling?"

*Trey? Who the hell is Trey?* Todd moved to the bar and mixed himself a drink. *Father? Brother?* The bottle of brandy slipped through his fingers and hit the tiled bar with a resounding crack as a third possibility occurred to him. *Husband?*

He thought back to his visit to her home. The address in Nichols Hills was a prestigious one—one he wasn't sure Leandra Gallagher could afford on her own. He remembered, too, how strange she had acted when she'd found him standing at her door. She'd practically mowed him down in her attempt to get out the door before pulling it behind her. And rings—she wore a diamond and a gold band on the ring finger of her left hand.

He glanced at the sofa where she sat with the phone receiver pressed tightly to her ear. Though she wore a watery smile, he could see by the worried expression beneath it that her gaiety was forced. He'd spent enough time in waiting rooms talking to family members of accident victims to recognize the look. Right now she was putting up a strong front for someone, but he knew the moment she hung up the phone she'd fall apart. A thin dam was all that held back the wall of emotions she suppressed.

Todd watched the slight trembling of her fingertips as she pressed them against her lips. She nodded mutely at something that was said, then choked out, "I love you, too, darling," before quickly hanging up the phone. Great heaving sobs shook her, and she gave in to them, dropping her face to her open palms.

Without hesitating, Todd moved to sit on the edge of the coffee table opposite her and pressed the glass of brandy he held into her hand.

"Here, drink this."

He waited until she'd taken a sip, then he handed her his handkerchief and watched while she dabbed at her tear-filled eyes. "You okay now?"

She started to nod, then shook her head as a new wave of tears flooded her eyes. Todd shifted to the sofa and pulled her to him, fitting her into the crook of his arm. "Can you tell me what happened?"

"Trey. It's Trey," she managed between broken sobs.

Tensing slightly, Todd asked, "Who's Trey?"

"My s-s-son. He—he broke his arm."

Todd pushed her out to hold her at arm's length, laughing in relief. "Your son broke his arm? Is that all?" The sudden flare of anger sparking in Leandra's eyes quickly squelched his laughter. He placed a hand on her shoulder. "I'm sorry. I didn't mean to laugh. It's just that . . . well, I expected something a lot more serious." *Like a husband*.

Leandra jerked away from him. "A broken arm to a little boy *is* serious!"

"And even more so to his mother. Especially when she's not there to take care of him."

Anger seeped out of Leandra, and she bowed her head, her action acknowledging her feelings of guilt. "I should have been there."

"You can't always be there for him."

"I know."

"Is this the first time he's broken anything?"

She nodded.

"It probably won't be the last."

"I know that, too." A shudder shook her shoulders, and Todd pulled her back against him, tucking her head beneath his chin.

He held out his opposite arm and rotated it for her inspection. "See this arm? It's been broken twice. Once when I fell from a tree and a second time when I made a dive for second base." He lifted his right leg. "And I broke this trying to reenact one of Evel Knievel's stunts on a motorcycle." Placing a finger beneath her chin, he turned her face to his. "My mother cried every time."

Tears streamed down Leandra's face, but this time there was laughter among the tears. To Todd, it was like the gift of a rainbow after a summer storm.

"Your poor mother. How did she ever manage to raise you?"

"I don't know, but she did. You'll manage, too."

Another shudder shook Leandra's shoulders beneath the weight of Todd's arm. "I guess. But I still wish I were there."

"We can go home if you like."

A deep sigh escaped Leandra's lips as she glanced up to look into Todd's eyes. In them she found understanding and compassion. "No. Mother assured me everything is fine, and Trey seemed to be as content as a puppy with a new bone. He said his principal went to the hospital with him and even signed his cast." She laughed lightly. "I'm the one who's a wreck."

"Who's your pediatrician?"

"Dr. Neeley. But he didn't set Trey's arm. Mother said it was such a nasty break Dr. Neeley called in an orthopedic surgeon. A Dr. Greenwold."

"Sidney." At Leandra's questioning look, he added, "Sidney Greenwold. I know him. Would it make you feel better if I called and talked to him?"

Leandra twisted around, unconsciously placing a hand on Todd's chest. "Oh, would you?"

Her fingertips sent tendrils of fire shooting through him. For a moment he was tempted to pull her into his arms and kiss her again. But he knew this wasn't the time. With great effort he suppressed the urge and instead picked up the phone and placed the call.

Beside Todd, Leandra nervously chewed her lip while she listened to his conversation with Dr. Greenwold. Hearing only one side of the discussion nearly drove her crazy. The medical terminology sounded like Greek, and Trey's condition, in her mind at least, worsened as she listened to its being so impersonally discussed in jargon.

When he finally hung up, Todd, using his own arm as a model, explained the nature of the injury and assured Leandra that after six weeks in a cast Trey's arm would be as good as new. Sidney had told him that physical therapy might be required for a few weeks after removal of the cast, but Todd held back that bit of information. There was no need to worry Leandra unnecessarily. The guilt she carried was enough of a burden for the time being.

Seeing Leandra's relief, Todd was glad he'd made the call. He'd told her they could go home if she wanted, and he would make good on his promise if she insisted on leaving Ixtapa. For some reason he couldn't quite explain, he didn't want the trip to end so abruptly. He wanted more time with her. That revelation alone shocked him. But he *had* promised. "Do you still want to go home?"

Leandra hesitated a moment, then shook her head. "No. I guess not." She blew out a long breath. "Mother's there, and God knows she's had enough experience dealing with broken bones." She laughed, and the sound was rich and husky after the tears shed earlier. "I have five brothers, and they've all broken more bones than I care to count."

"Five brothers!"

Leandra laughed again. She was accustomed to the effect the size of her family usually had on people. "Yes, and three sisters."

Todd absorbed that bit of information in silence. To him a large family had always signified a happy one—something he'd always wanted for himself. He wondered if Leandra's family had been happy and if she'd been able to carry that happiness over into her own home.

And what of Trey's father? He wanted to ask but didn't know quite how to broach the subject. He chose the round-about method and asked instead about her son. "How old is Trey?"

"Seven."

"Do you have any other children?"

The smile slowly melted from Leandra's face. "No. Only Trey."

"Oh." Todd plucked at the crease in his cotton duck slacks, then tilted his face to glance at Leandra. "Since you're here, I assume you're divorced from Trey's father."

Though it was hard, Leandra forced herself to meet his questioning look. "No." She watched his eyes widen in surprise. "Trey doesn't have a father." Quickly she stood and picked up the glass of brandy and carried it to the bar.

*Why was she so damn tightfisted with any subject that dealt with her personal life?* Todd wondered in frustration. While he watched her cross the room, he sorted through the scattered bits of information she'd revealed to him.

A mother. That one thought fixed in his mind. Leandra Gallagher, a mother. And a single mother at that. That might be the reason she so carefully guarded her private life.

But Todd wanted to know about Trey's father, for he

couldn't believe any man would willingly walk away from a child he'd produced.

"You've raised your son alone, then?"

"Yes."

"Why?"

Leandra's mind flashed back to those grueling months of indecision when she'd fretted over what to do: abortion versus adoption versus rearing a child on her own. She'd quickly eliminated abortion as a possibility. The baby was a part of her . . . as well as a part of the man who'd fathered it. Even though its conception had been an accident and one the father wasn't willing to share responsibility for, she knew she couldn't end the life she'd had a part in beginning.

That had left her only two options: adoption or raising the child alone.

Adoption, she'd been advised by both her parents and her doctor, was the only realistic decision. After all, Leandra was only seventeen. She had no high school degree or means of supporting herself, much less a child. By placing the baby with adoptive parents, she would be ensuring the child's welfare.

In the beginning, she had succumbed to their guidance, but with each passing month as the baby swelled within her, her confidence in her decision began to waver. At the first flutter of movement, she knew adoption wasn't the answer. No matter what sacrifices would be required of her, she was determined to keep her baby.

Seven years later, she still didn't regret the decision.

"Because he was my child, and I wasn't willing to have an abortion or put him up for adoption."

"I can understand that, but why didn't you ask the boy's father for help?"

Frustration built within her until she thought she'd either

scream or burst into hysterical laughter. She had never discussed Trey's father with anyone, not even her parents. Now here she was talking about it openly—and with Todd Stillman of all people.

Instead of knuckling under to the emotions bursting within her, Leandra lifted her gaze to Todd's and met his questioning glance squarely. "I tried."

"And?"

"Suffice it to say, his family didn't want anything to do with a bastard child."

The challenging look in her eyes drew admiration from Todd. His thoughts shifted to wondering what kind of man could walk away from Leandra Gallagher. A foolish one, he decided as he watched her rinse out the brandy glass.

Curious to know what part, if any, the boy's father played in their lives, he asked, "Does Trey ever see his father?"

"No."

"That's too bad."

Leandra finished drying the glass and folded the bar towel and placed it beside the sink. "You don't miss what you've never had."

Todd thought of his relationship with his own father. Eight years of estrangement lay between them like a deep, gaping cavern, keeping them apart, neither willing to take the first step to close that gap. There were times when Todd longed for the closeness they'd once shared. He had memories of summers filled with father and son camp-outs, Little League baseball, fishing trips, and family vacations. But those memories were all before his father had begun his wandering ways. What memories would *her* son have to reflect on? Pensively, he replied, "Maybe."

"What?" Leandra asked in a surprised voice as she wheeled to look at him.

"Never mind," he said with a resigned sigh as he stood and stretched. It wasn't his place to tell Leandra what her son was missing. That realization would come soon enough. "Butch and Ben want us to meet them at Carlos and Charlie's for a drink at nine."

Leandra disappeared behind the bar that separated them as she bent to replace the bottle of brandy. "I'm really rather tired. If you don't mind, I think I'll pass."

"You sure?"

"Yes," she said as she straightened. "But you go ahead. I'm going to call Trey again in a little bit, then call it a night."

With Todd gone, Leandra found herself alone in the suite for the first time during their stay in Ixtapa. Taking advantage of the privacy, she took a long hot shower, washed her hair, and changed into her nightgown and robe before calling home again to check on Trey.

As Leandra had predicted, her mother had everything under control. She'd made Trey's favorite meal, hamburgers and French fries, and had even baked him chocolate chip cookies, which he noisily munched while he talked to Leandra. Their conversation hadn't lasted long. His grandmother had bought Trey a new video game, and he was anxious to get back to it.

It hurt a little to realize her son didn't miss her or need her, especially since she needed him so much. He was everything to her and had been since the day of his birth. She'd centered her life, her very existence, on him to the exclusion of all else.

Even if she'd wanted one, a social life for a single parent was difficult to maintain. Work, household responsibilities, and taking care of Trey filled her days. There was never time for much else.

Feeling a little lonely in the empty suite, Leandra sought the company of the open balcony and the comforting sound of the sea. She relaxed against the padded cushions of the lounge chair. Far below her she could hear the murmur of voices. Probably couples taking advantage of the secluded beach and the moonlit night, she thought wistfully.

Mexico had certainly fulfilled all the pictorial promises portrayed by the travel brochures she'd studied before her trip. It was easy to become enchanted with the beauty and romance of this sleepy village.

A soft wind blew spray from the sea across her face, and she closed her eyes as she ran her tongue across her lips and tasted the salt. It drew a pleasant memory, one of diving deep beneath the ocean's surface earlier that day with Todd at her side, guiding her. He'd shown her fish in colors that challenged those of the rainbow and had retrieved pieces of coral from the bottom of the ocean's floor as gifts for her.

He had taught her the art of snorkeling—how to breathe through the rubber mouthpiece, how to skim across the ocean's surface while watching the sea life through protective goggles. He'd shown her the magic and the mystery of the ocean's depths with a patience and a kindness that surprised her.

Before the trip, she'd been determined to maintain an emotional distance from him. Once burned was enough for her. But through their forced proximity she had found him a comfortable companion. Easygoing, fun to be with, and considerate. To that list of adjectives she could add handsome, virile, passionate, but she calmly thrust aside those thoughts.

She didn't want to like him. She wanted only to survive the trip, then forget him.

She pulled her thin robe closer to her breasts and snuggled deeper into the cushions. Without meaning to, she drifted off to sleep remembering the secure feel of Todd's fingers laced through hers as they'd walked hand in hand along the beach of Ixtapa Island.

Todd sat at the bar, idly twirling a miniature paper umbrella around the edge of a scooped-out pineapple shell. Butch and Ben had left over an hour ago to check out more of Ixtapa's nightlife for their program. He'd declined their invitation to join them. Why, he wasn't sure.

"Another drink, señor?"

Todd glanced up at the bartender, then at the empty pineapple shell in front of him. How many had he polished off? Three or was it four? Oh, what the hell. Who was counting? "Yeah, one more."

Spinning around to face away from the bar, he leaned back and rested his elbows against the tiled counter while he idly scanned the nightclub. Couples swayed and churned on the packed dance floor, illuminated by flashing strobe lights as they danced to the pulsing beat of the marimba band. As he watched the dancers, he wondered what it would be like to dance with Leandra—to hold her in his arms, to feel her body pressed against his.

He knew the pleasure of walking along the beach with her, her slender fingers threaded through his. He knew the joy of her laughter when she'd felt the first tug of the ocean's tide against her bare feet. He knew the thrill of watching the excitement build on her face when she'd landed her first fish.

At first those responses had been forced by the ever-present camera crew. But as the day wore on, those same emotions came instinctively and with them a need to touch her, to see the beauty and enchantment of her smile again.

He hadn't intended to kiss her. But when she had turned to him, her gaze full of wonder at the sun's majestic display, he had forgotten about the McCain brothers and the camera and thought only of satisfying his own selfish needs.

Now he knew what it was like to kiss her. To feel the velvety softness of her lips on his. To feel the answering warmth of her response. To—

"Six thousand pesos, señor."

The sound of the bartender's heavy Spanish accent jerked Todd's wandering thoughts from Leandra and plopped him down in the noisy nightclub. He whirled around on his bar stool, pulling his wallet from the back pocket of his slacks. In his haste to pay the bartender, he dumped the contents of his wallet onto the bar. Among the scattered bills lay Leandra's faded blue check.

Todd picked up the check and smoothed it open, looking again at his father's scrawled writing, then flipped it over to study Leandra's feminine signature.

The resentment that flooded him each time he looked at the check was surprisingly absent. Something had changed. *But what?* he wondered as he carefully refolded the check. The check was still there, proof enough of Leandra's involvement with his father. And when questioned, she hadn't denied her relationship with Robert Stillman. In fact, she'd verified Todd's suspicions by telling him his father had tried to buy her off. Yet, if any resentment remained, it was directed at his father for his callous behavior to such a young and impressionable girl.

The fact that Leandra had never cashed the check raised Todd's opinion of her a few notches. So she isn't a gold digger, he concluded, tapping the check against the tiled bar. She'd been a young, naive girl who'd made a mistake by placing her trust in an older man.

In a way, he was almost glad Leandra had been involved with his father. If she hadn't, Todd knew he might never have met her himself.

He slipped the check back into his wallet and shoved it deep into his pocket. He'd had his reasons for not wanting to make this trip—justifiable reasons. But somehow those reasons didn't seem as important now.

Without ever taking a sip of the piña colada the bartender had placed in front of him, Todd slipped off the bar stool and headed back to the hotel.

Something tickled at Leandra's cheek, and she sleepily brushed a hand in the direction of the irritating sensation. It touched her again. Her ear this time. She twisted away from it, turning onto her side and curling her hands beneath her cheek. A deep sigh escaped her as she nestled more comfortably into the cushions.

"Wake up, Sleeping Beauty," a soft voice whispered.

Her conscious mind warred with the whispered urging. She was sleeping too well to want to end her dreams.

Something warm played across her cheek, then feathered across her lips.

Slowly, she opened her eyes. For a moment it was as if her dream had taken form, for Todd's face was mere inches above hers. In slow motion she lifted a tentative finger to his face, then jerked back when her hand touched warm flesh. Suddenly wide awake, she pressed her head back into the cushions as she eyed him warily. "What are you doing?"

"Kissing Sleeping Beauty awake."

His breath smelled of coconuts and rum. "You're drunk."

"No, I'm not. I've only been drunk once in my life. A very disappointing evening, as I recall. I had hoped to blot out the past, but all I succeeded in forgetting was that one night. I don't intend to forget this one, Sleeping Beauty."

"I'm not Sleeping Beauty."

"And I'm not Prince Charming," he replied, arching one eyebrow meaningfully at her.

He was so close Leandra could see only his face. But it was his mouth she focused on. One side of it curled up in a boyish grin. She watched in shock as that lopsided grin drifted down toward her. His lips touched hers, retreated, then touched hers again.

Slender coils of heat spiraled through her body. Resolved to maintain a safe distance, she placed a restraining hand on his chest. "I'm awake now, Prince Charming. The kiss isn't necessary."

Bracing himself on the arms of the lounge chair, Todd smiled lazily down at her. "Unnecessary, but definitely worth repeating.

With her hand still pressed against his chest, she asked, "What time is it?"

"After midnight."

"Did you have fun at Carlos and Charlie's?" She sat up straighter in the chair and tried to put as much space as possible between herself and Todd. But when she scooted away from him, the fabric of her robe caught on the edge of the chair.

Fascinated, Todd watched the thin straps of her gown slip to the middle of her upper arm. "No," he murmured in a husky voice before dipping down to nibble at the soft skin on her shoulder.

Leandra sucked in a breath as his cool lips touched the warmth of her sun-kissed skin. "Oh? Why not?" she managed to choke out.

He lifted his gaze to hers, his steel-gray eyes like molten

silver as he focused on her. "Because of you." His touch was gentle as he traced her lower lip with the ball of his thumb. "I couldn't get you off my mind. You're beautiful, you know that? So beautiful." His gaze drifted to her hair, which hung full and loose to her shoulders, and he thought how much younger she looked with it down. "You should let your hair down more often, Leandra."

From his tone she suspected he meant more than the simple style of her hair. Self-consciously, she moved her hand to the wind-dried wisps. "I must look like a ragamuffin. I showered while you were gone and came out here to let my hair dry. But I fell asleep, and—"

He caught her hand and pulled it to his lips, silencing her. "You look wonderful. Trust me," he said as he moved her arm to drape across his shoulder.

Her arm tensed until it felt as if it were cast in iron. *Trust what?* she asked herself. *Him or his opinion of her looks?* She suspected he meant the broader sense. But trust was something that didn't come easily for her. It was something sacred that could only be earned. Could she trust Todd Stillman? Could she trust herself with him?

"You do trust me, don't you?" he asked as he smoothed the tips of his fingers across her wrinkled brow.

Leandra's pent-up breath whooshed out of her. "No . . . I mean, yes. Oh, I don't know what I mean," she finished feebly.

"Today at the beach you trusted me."

"What?"

"You didn't jump when I touched you. You even let me hold your hand."

Leandra felt her pulse quicken. "But that was all part of the act. I was just playing my part."

"Were you playing your part when we watched the sunset and I kissed you?"

Heat flushed her cheeks, and she looked away from his knowing gaze.

"I didn't think so," he said as a half-smile played across his face. "Why don't you admit it, Leandra? You're attracted to me, too."

"I am not!"

"Yes, you are. I can prove it."

He silenced her denial with his lips. Stubbornly, she pushed against his chest and tried to twist away, but he held her firmly in his grasp. Where his first kiss had been tentative and unsure, this one burned hot against her lips, as if he were confident of her response.

When she continued to struggle against him, his kiss turned to nibbled entreaties. "Let go, Leandra. Don't fight me anymore." His lips rained stinging kisses across her face and down her slender neck.

Drowning in the torrential shower of his persuasive kisses, Leandra let her resistance gradually dissolve. Her fingers no longer pushed him away but instead clutched at the soft fabric of his shirt. With a muffled groan, Todd dropped to his knees beside the lounge chair and pulled her hard against him. His mouth slanted across hers, smothering her in his quest to know her, to taste her.

Years of loneliness she hadn't been aware of until that moment had her clinging to him, opening her senses to all this man could evoke. Her lips parted with a sigh, and he quickly slipped his tongue between them, bringing to her the taste of the coconuts that before had been only an enticing scent in the air. The rush of the ocean's waves on the beach echoed the rhythm of their passion as his mouth rocked over hers.

His fingers found the back of her neck, then climbed higher to tangle in her hair, the palms of his hands moving to cup her face.

Following his example, Leandra threaded her fingers up through his hair, then let them drift down, tracing the sharp planes of his cheeks and jawline, before resting them lightly on his chest. In the open V of his shirt, her fingertips rippled across the dark hair swirling on his chest.

"Leandra."

The sound of her name, whispered against her fevered skin, was headier than any wine. It was like the music of the sea, enchanting in its hypnotic call.

For a moment, it was as if she'd been caught by a tidal wave, trapped beneath its churning waters. Immersed below its drowning depths, she emerged to grab a breath of air, then was pulled once again to flounder in breathless anticipation.

She felt as if she were suffocating, but if this was death, she welcomed it.

Allowing the passionate wave to carry her, she rose on its crest, floating on the pinnacle, glorying in the sensations—then plummeted to the bottom of the ocean's floor.

Bereft, she opened her eyes and found Todd braced above her in the same fashion as he'd been when she first awoke. If not for the raspy sound of his labored breathing and the passionate flush coloring his cheeks, she'd have thought this only a continuation of her dream.

One side of his mouth curved up into a half-smile. "I said you could trust me. Much more of this and I'm afraid I won't be able to trust myself."

"Maybe I should go in now."

"Not just yet." He caught her hand and pulled her to stand in front of him, draping his arms loosely at her waist. Soft music from the lounge several floors below floated up to them.

"When I was at the nightclub, I kept wondering what it would be like to dance with you."

He tightened his arms around her, pulling her flush against him, and began to sway, matching his movements to the rhythm of the soft music. "Dance with me now, Leandra."

Without waiting for her reply, he began to move slowly toward the balcony's edge, carefully guiding her around the lounge chair with gentle pressure from his fingertips. Relaxing against him, Leandra circled his neck with her arms and rested her cheek in the soft curve of his shoulder.

Beyond and above them, thousands of glittering stars seemed to wink their approval of Leandra's choice in dance partners. Sighing her contentment, she closed her eyes, knowing no nightclub could equal the beauty of their dance floor. Bougainvillaeas permeated the air with their intoxicating floral scent, and she breathed deeply of the fragrance while her robe brushed lightly against the plant's fragile blooms.

Cheek to cheek, heart to heart, they danced around the small patio with Todd adroitly maneuvering them between the patio furniture and the small private pool. His touch, first warm at her waist, grew hot, searing her skin through the light fabric of her robe.

His steps slowed, then stopped altogether, yet his body continued to sway against hers.

"Leandra," he whispered against her hair before slowly drawing away from her. His hands moved to cup her elbows, holding her at arm's length while his fevered gaze met hers.

Moonlight spun a web of enchantment around them, draping them in its silver-white glow. The fairy tale quality of the evening made Leandra feel as if she were indeed Sleeping Beauty and Todd her Prince Charming. Sensations slumbering deep within her had been awakened by his kiss. Now her body yearned for the feel of his arms, her lips for his touch.

She lifted a hand to his face, her fingers lightly tracing the line of his jaw, each feature so achingly familiar, yet so foreign. As she looked into the depths of his gray eyes, Leandra realized there could be no happily-ever-afters for her. Not with Todd Stillman. For them, there would only be this moment out of time.

"Leandra? What is it? You look so sad."

"Nothing. Just hold me, Todd. Please."

He gathered her into his arms, holding her close, his lips pressed against her temple. A shudder passed through her body.

Todd caught her chin and tilted it up until her lips met his. For Leandra, never was the taste of revenge so bitter as when his lips touched hers again.

## FIVE

Unable to sleep, Todd opened the shuttered doors leading from his bedroom to the balcony and stepped out into the moonlit night. No light peeked through the slats of Leandra's door at the opposite end of the patio. Obviously she didn't suffer the insomnia that plagued him.

Though his body ached from lack of rest, sleep wouldn't come. Troubled thoughts whirled through his mind. Thoughts centered on Leandra.

Before making this trip, four days and three nights in Ixtapa had sounded like an eternity. Now, their last night here, he wondered where the time had gone.

On reflection, because of their late arrival, the first night had been a wash, although they'd made up for it with a full schedule the following day. Deep-sea fishing, snorkeling, sunbathing, and lunch on Ixtapa Island. He had tried to take advantage of every activity the small village offered. Butch and Ben had been careful not to invade upon Todd's time with Leandra, but the constant whir of the camera had been reminder enough of their presence.

At first, Todd hadn't minded their company, but as the

day wore on, he began to wish for time alone with Leandra. At the auction and during their subsequent meetings before the trip, he'd thought her cool and aloof. The ice queen, he remembered with a rueful laugh.

Mexico had shown him a different side of her personality, totally changing his opinion. Watching her undisguised fascination as they traveled through the remote countryside had been like watching a child on Christmas morning. Every change in scenery, every activity they'd been involved in had been a gift that Leandra opened with bright-eyed enthusiasm.

Todd leaned back against the balcony's edge, his thoughts reflective as his gaze drifted around the private patio. The climax of that first full day, at least in his estimation, had been when he'd found Leandra sleeping here and had awakened her with a kiss. They'd shared something special that night as they'd danced beneath the stars. Whether it was a product of the magical evening or true emotion, he wasn't sure, but it was definitely something.

For the most part, that same special something had carried over into today.

While sightseeing and shopping in Ixtapa and the neighboring village of Zihuatanejo, Leandra had appeared lighthearted and gay, at ease with him. But there had been moments when he'd caught her unaware and found her staring forlornly into space. When questioned, she had immediately pasted on a bright smile and assured him nothing was wrong.

In his heart, he knew she was lying.

He frowned at the stars studding the dark velvety sky. Something had happened last night when the music had ended their dance, something he couldn't explain. When she'd asked him to hold her, he'd felt the weight of her sadness, the desperation in her embrace.

*What*? his mind cried out in the silence of the night. What had happened to steal the magic they'd shared?

He wanted to wash away the melancholy, to fix whatever hurt. But he had no more clue now than before as to what caused her pain. If he had, he'd vanquish that which tormented her . . . just to see the beauty of her smile again.

The following morning, still tired as a result of his sleepless night, Todd made arrangements for a taxi to take them to the airport while Leandra finished packing.

The ride to the airport in the neighboring village of Zihuatanejo seemed shorter than the one taken on their arrival. But then, now that it was time to leave, everything seemed to have speeded up—even his heartbeat, which thundered like the hooves of a herd of wild horses against his rib cage.

Butch and Ben had planned a later flight home, which left Todd and Leandra to board the plane alone. Both pensive, they sat in silence, each dreading the moment the plane touched the runway at Will Rogers Airport.

When the pilot announced the final approach to Oklahoma City, Todd, unable to express the myriad of emotions running deep within him, laced his fingers through Leandra's and squeezed reassuringly. She clung to him as the landing wheels bounced against the runway, her eyes bright with unshed tears.

That feeling of dread stayed with them until they claimed their luggage and loaded it into Todd's car. Then, at last, he turned to her, his face taut with emotion. "Leandra, I don't want this to be the end. I want to see you again."

For a moment, wings of joy soared within her, blinding her to all else. Although she knew it was impossible, she didn't want this time to end any more than he did.

He tightened his grip on her hand. "I want to meet your son. Get to know him, too."

Meet her son? The past swept over her, slowly melting her elation. How would she ever explain Trey to Todd? Or Todd to Trey for that matter? "I don't know," she hedged before pulling away to climb into the car. "School and extracurricular activities keep him pretty busy."

Puzzled by her unexpected evasion, Todd closed her door and circled the car to his side. *It had to be Trey*, Todd decided as he climbed in beside her. Every time the boy's name was mentioned, Leandra, like a turtle, withdrew into her protective shell.

Twisting in the seat to face her, he placed a restraining hand on her shoulder. "Listen, Leandra. If you'd rather I didn't meet Trey yet, that's okay. But if you don't want to see me, I'd like to know."

"Oh, no. It's not that." Leandra bit nervously at her lower lip, then dipped her head to escape Todd's questioning gaze. "It's just that . . . well, Trey is . . ." Her voice drifted off, for she was unable to name the reason for her reluctance.

"Are you worried how Trey would accept me?"

"Well, yes . . ."

"Is that all?" Todd laughed in relief, slapping the steering wheel of the car. "Hell, Leandra, I'm great with kids! I have a niece and nephew who will gladly provide references for me."

Leandra's answering smile was weak. If it were only that easy, she thought wistfully.


"Trey?" Leandra called as she pushed open the massive front door. Walking quickly beneath the double arches opening to the rear hallway, she called again, "Tre-ey."

Todd watched her disappear behind a swinging door, then reappear moments later, a note clutched in her hand.

"It seems they've gone to take Mother home." She tossed the note dejectedly to the black marble-topped table in the entry hall.

Catching her by the hand, Todd pulled her into his arms, his voice teasing as he asked, "What were you expecting? A welcome home party?"

"No. But I thought he would at least be here to meet me."

"You'll see him soon enough."

"I know." Leandra gave in to the warmth Todd's chest offered and the comforting sound of his heartbeat. "But I've missed the little demon."

"Since he's gone, why don't you have dinner with me?" he whispered against her hair.

Leandra felt her resolve weakening. Trey. She had to keep her mind focused on Trey. "I couldn't. Not my first night home. Trey should be home soon and will be anxious to hear about my trip."

Todd frowned. "This week is booked solid because of our trip, and I'm on call this weekend. How about Friday of next week? We could have dinner or something."

"It's rather difficult to plan that far in advance."

Todd's frown deepened, but he refused to accept any more evasion. "I'll call you. Just don't make any more plans until you hear from me. Okay?"

Leandra leaned back in his arms and looked into the depths of his silver-gray eyes. Within them she saw the same steely determination she'd glimpsed several times during their trip together. A tiny seed of hope grew within her. If she took things slowly, allowed their feelings for each other to forge into something stronger, maybe things could work out. But she wouldn't, couldn't risk involving Trey until she was sure.

That resolved in her mind, she nodded her agreement before succumbing to the comforting strength of his embrace once again.

In the days that followed the return from her trip, Leandra gradually slipped back into her daily routine, although it was a difficult adjustment after the slow pace of Mexico. But with her responsibilities to both Trey and John, she wasn't given much choice in the matter.

Her third night home it was after eleven when she finally climbed into bed. Almost immediately, the telephone rang, startling her. She grabbed for it, catching it before Trey or John awakened.

"Hello."

"Hi. Were you sleeping?"

A warmth seeped through her at the sound of Todd's husky voice. "Not yet. I'd just turned out my light."

"You're in bed then?"

Leandra couldn't stop the smile building on her face. She hadn't seen or heard from Todd since their return, but he had constantly been in her thoughts. "Yes."

'Wish I were there."

"Oh? And what would you do if you were?" Leandra asked teasingly.

"Sleep. I'm exhausted."

She laughed at his unexpected answer. "I think I've just been insulted."

"Hardly. Remind me to never take a vacation again."

"Why's that?" Leandra asked as she slipped beneath the covers, thoroughly enjoying the sound of Todd's voice in the intimate darkness of her bedroom.

"Inevitably I have twice as much to do when I return."

"Rough day?"

"Three rough days. How about you? Have you acclimatized to the fast-paced life of the United States?"

"Almost. It's good to be home, although I do miss the sound of the ocean when I go to sleep at night."

"Yeah, me too. Among other things."

Leandra arched one eyebrow, her smile deepening. "Oh? And what else have you missed?"

"You." She thought she heard the whisper of a deep sigh before he added, "I wish we could have had more time."

Thoughtfully, Leandra smoothed the covers on her bed. "Oh, I don't know. Mexico was wonderful, but there was such a fairy tale quality to everything there. Maybe it's best we are back in reality."

"How about a little bit of reality tomorrow night?"

"What?" she laughed, having difficulty keeping up with his train of thought.

"Dinner. My place."

Leandra caught her lower lip between her teeth, then replied hesitantly, "I don't have much free time."

"I'll take what you have."

She smiled at his persistence. "Trey has Cub Scouts from 6:30 to 8:30 tomorrow night and—"

"Great! I'll pick you up at 6:45."

"No! I mean . . . let me think a minute. I'll need to drop Trey at his meeting, then be back in time to pick him up. That would only give us about an hour and a half at the most."

"It doesn't matter. I just want to see you."

"Could I meet you somewhere?"

"Why don't you drop off Trey, then come by the hospital and pick me up? We could grab a hamburger or something and have a picnic in the car out by Lake Hefner."

"Okay. But where do I pick you up?"

"At the emergency entrance to Mercy Hospital. I'll watch for you."

"Fine. I'll see you about 6:45 then?"

"Okay."

There was a long stretch of silence, their breathing the only sound crossing the telephone lines. Finally, Todd broke the silence. "Well, I guess I'd better let you go. It's pretty late."

"Yes, I guess it is."

There was another pause, as each was reluctant to end the call. Todd chuckled. "This reminds me of high school. Tell you what. On the count of three, we both hang up. Ready? One . . . two . . . three." Silence. "You didn't hang up."

Leandra laughed. "Neither did you."

"Okay, I promise I will this time. One . . . two . . . three." Click.

Leandra listened to the dial tone hum a moment while she continued to cradle the phone at her ear. He had called her. And he had missed her. That was a good sign, wasn't it? *Oh, Leandra*, she chided as she stretched across the bed to replace the receiver. *For heaven's sake, it's only a date*.

But dates for Leandra Gallagher were rare, and a date with Todd Stillman . . . well, she'd never actually had a *real* date with him.

The following afternoon after work she changed clothes three times before finally deciding on a bulky cotton sweater and corduroy slacks to wear to meet him. The entire time she was dressing she worried. *What would they talk about? What would they do? Eat, you silly goose*, she told herself as she struggled to pull on a pair of flats.

She stepped in front of the dresser mirror to check her

appearance. Pasting on a casual smile, she said, "Hello, Todd," then frowned at her reflection. "Ugh! That's pitiful."

Several more practiced greetings were made, then discarded as being too formal, too personal, or just plain boring. She paced back and forth across her room, then stopped before the mirror again. Tossing back her hair, she smiled and said, "Hi, Todd. It's good to see you again." She paused for a moment, weighing the effect of her words. "Perfect," she declared to her reflection. "Friendly but not gushy."

"Mom, who are you talking to?"

Leandra wheeled around. Trey stood in the doorway, staring at her, a puzzled look on his face. Embarrassed, she grabbed her jacket and purse. "No one, sweetheart. Do you have your Cub Scout manual?"

"Yeah." Trey ducked as Leandra attempted to comb her fingers through his mussed hair. "Hurry up," he called over his shoulder as he hurried down the hall. "I don't want to miss the refreshments."

Trey made it to the Scout meeting on time, and at exactly 6:45, Leandra pulled into the emergency entrance to Mercy Hospital. All her practiced greetings flew from her mind when she saw Todd standing on the ramp in front of the emergency room's sliding glass doors. The wind whipped around him, billowing his leather bomber jacket and realigning the part in his hair. When he saw her, he grinned and lifted his hand in a wave as he loped down the steps to meet her.

For a split second, her nerves got the better of her and she was tempted to drive away before it was too late— before she lost her heart to this man. But then the door opened and Todd slipped inside, the wind sneaking in with him and stealing the warmth of the car's interior.

His welcoming smile kicked up the speed of her already pounding heart and slowly unraveled the knots that had twisted tight in her stomach all day.

It was then that she realized it was already too late. Her heart belonged to Todd Stillman.

"You wore your hair down." He leaned across the seat and slipped his hand beneath the weight of her hair, pulling her toward him until her lips met his. "I like it this way." He touched his lips to hers again before releasing her and relaxing against the seat. "I'm starving. How about you?"

Painfully aware she had been holding her breath since the moment his fingers had touched the bare skin above her sweater, she carefully released it before she replied, "Famished. What are you hungry for?"

Todd chuckled mischievously. "Are we talking in terms of food?"

"Yes."

"Well, you choose. You're driving."

Knowing full well she wouldn't be able to eat a bite, Leandra drove to Trey's favorite fast-food restaurant. She pulled up to the drive-in window and ordered hamburgers and French fries. With the sack of food warming the seat between them, she followed Todd's directions to a secluded area on the shore of Lake Hefner.

Dusk settled around them while they ate, and in the waning light the wind died down, turning the lake's surface to glass. Leandra nibbled at her hamburger, too conscious of Todd sitting beside her to make much of a dent in it.

He eyed her bag of French fries. "Do you mind?" he asked as he plucked one from the bag and popped it into his mouth.

She laughed. "Would it matter?"

"No. Like I said, I'm starving."

He picked up her sack of fries and slumped lower in the seat. "I love the lake at this time of night. It's so peaceful."

Leandra looked out across the still water at the lights bordering the far shore, noticing for the first time the serenity of their location. "Yes, it is."

"After being cooped up all day at the hospital, it feels good to get out."

"Do you mind it much? Being cooped up, I mean."

"No. I love my work. Can't imagine doing anything else." Todd glanced at her. "Want to take a walk?"

"Sure."

At the hood of the car, Todd laced his fingers through Leandra's and guided her down a dim path along the lake's shore. Debris washed up on the bank crackled beneath their feet. His fingers rubbed against the band of gold circling her left ring finger. He stopped and lifted their hands between them.

"Why do you wear these?" he asked, pushing at the rings with his thumb.

Even in the cool night air, Leandra felt a blush warm her cheeks. "To avoid awkward questions."

"Like what?"

"Like why isn't the mother of a seven-year-old boy married?"

Todd looked from the rings to Leandra. "Lots of people have children out of wedlock. Why is it important to you for people to think you're married?"

"Not for me. For Trey. I've never wanted anyone to call him a bastard."

"Would they really call him that?"

"Not in so many words. Wearing the rings helps."

Todd noted the determined lift of her chin and the defensive gleam in her eye. It drew a renewed respect from him and an even stronger desire to protect her.

"Did Trey's father give them to you?"

"No. The wedding band was my grandmother's, and the diamond is a cubic zirconium." At Todd's confused expression, Leandra added, "Paste. I couldn't afford anything else."

She looked at the diamond ring and the narrow gold band that she'd worn for almost seven years. When questioned, she had never lied to anyone about her past, but she had never told anyone the whole truth either. She'd always allowed people to make their own assumptions with what scanty information she provided. Wearing the rings had never bothered her before, but now the weight of the lie it symbolized seemed unusually heavy.

Shivers chased down her spine, and she pulled her hand from Todd's and hugged her arms beneath her breasts. She didn't want to discuss this topic. Not yet, anyway.

Todd slipped his arm around her shoulder, cradling her against his side. "Cold?"

"A little."

"Want my jacket?"

"No. Just the sleeve."

Todd chuckled and pulled her into his arms, hugging her close to his chest. "How about both of them?"

Slipping her hands beneath his jacket to circle his waist, she nestled against him. "This is heaven."

"Not quite. Someday I'll show you heaven." He leaned back and tilted her chin until her blue gaze met his gray one. His tone was teasing, but the smoky hue of his eyes was dead serious. "I've missed you. That's hard for me to admit, but I have."

She tightened her hold on his waist. "I've missed you, too."

For a moment, time hung in suspense as they stared deep into each other's eyes. The gentle lapping of the water against the bank beside them reminded Leandra of Mexico and the sound of the ocean, then carried her memory farther back to another time when she'd stood on the edge of a lake wrapped in Todd's arms. Then, as now, she saw the flicker of pain and uncertainty in his eyes.

Not understanding it but wanting to erase that which haunted him, Leandra rose on her toes until her face was even with his. She touched her lips to his, then withdrew a fraction. Heat misted his eyes as he dipped his head to find her lips again. The kiss deepened, softened to a tender exploration, then deepened once again, sending Leandra's nerves skittering beneath her skin.

Abruptly, he peeled his lips from hers and held her at arm's length, his breathing ragged as he gazed into her startled face. "I don't know the first thing about properly courting a woman and really don't give a damn about learning. For the past eight years I've been buried in medical school and never dated the same woman twice. My life isn't my own. I've just opened a surgical practice and it demands ninety-nine-point-nine percent of my time and attention. The other one tenth of a percent is yours, if you want it."

Leandra stood spellbound, listening, her heart lodged in her throat. When he finished, she took a long breath, then slowly blew it out while he watched, waiting impatiently for her answer.

Her gaze never left his face. In her eyes Todd saw the emotions at war within her. The gauntlet had been thrown. It was up to her to take it up or walk away.

When at last she whispered, "I'll take it," he scooped her up in his arms, crushing her against him as he spun them around in a dizzying circle.

\* \* \*

Over the next several days, Leandra soon discovered how minuscule one tenth of a percent actually was. But she accepted what time Todd could squeeze out of his tight schedule and adjusted her own timetable to mesh with his. Coffee in the hospital cafeteria before work and Leandra's brown-bag lunch shared in the hospital's parking lot were more often than not their dates. Fifteen minutes stolen here, thirty minutes there. For some it wouldn't have been enough, but for Leandra it was.

*And so what if their meetings weren't always in the most romantic settings?* she thought defensively. Simply being with Todd filled her life with more excitement than she'd ever known.

Suspecting the lunch they shared might be the only meal Todd would eat each day, she began to pack more food to compensate for his appetite and included fresh fruits and vegetables to ensure he received at least one balanced meal a day.

Her efforts didn't go unnoticed by Todd. On Wednesday noon, after nearly a week of brown-bagging it, Todd watched Leandra clear away the remains of their lunch from the front seat of her car. He stilled her movements with a touch of his hand. "Paybacks. Tonight I'll cook dinner for you."

Leandra met his soft gaze, a mischievous twinkle in her eye. "You can cook?"

"Ever heard of the Galloping Gourmet?"

"Yes, and he doesn't look anything like you."

"Looks can be deceiving."

"Not *that* deceiving."

Ignoring her skeptical look, he lifted her hair away from her face with the tip of his index finger and leaned close, his breath blowing warm against her skin. "I think we'll start with clam vichyssoise or perhaps a Caesar salad with my own special dressing.'' He touched his lips to the delicate curve of her neck, and shivers chased down her spine. ''Then, for the entrée, steak *au poivre*, accompanied by a lightly fruited pilaf. And dessert . . . ah, yes, dessert,'' he murmured as he nibbled his way up to her lips. ''Bananas flambé.''

Leandra batted his hand away as she laughed. ''In other words you're offering me steaks on the grill and a tossed salad.''

''Only if you can make the salad.''

She laughed again. ''It's a date.''

# SIX

Smiling as she remembered the elaborate menu Todd had described, Leandra stepped up onto the front porch of his home. She turned and waved at Mrs. Brumbelow, watching until John's housekeeper disappeared from sight. When she turned again, she noticed the front door stood wide open. She stepped back and glanced up at the house number. Yes, it was the address Todd had given her. But why was the door open? She took a cautious step inside.

"Todd?" Her voice echoed in the empty living room. There wasn't a stick of furniture in sight. Goose bumps popped up on her arms as she scanned the room, searching for some sign of occupancy. Curiosity surpassed her apprehension, and she moved farther into the room. She hadn't taken two steps when the front door slammed behind her. She wheeled, panic clawing its way up her throat.

From behind her she heard footsteps coming from the back of the house. Convinced she was at the wrong address and not prepared to meet whoever was coming, she thought only of escape. She bolted for the door, but just as her hand twisted on the knob, a man's hand closed over hers. A scream built in her throat, and she whirled around, flattening herself against the wood-paneled door.

She pressed a hand against her chest when she saw Todd standing in front of her. "Todd! You scared the life out of me!"

"I'm sorry. Didn't you hear me call your name?"

Leandra took a deep, steadying breath. "No. But my heart was pounding so loudly, I'm not sure I could have heard anything." Feeling rather silly at being spooked so easily, she began to explain, her words tumbling out in fragmented thoughts. "The front door was wide open. I rang the doorbell, but when you didn't answer . . . I saw the empty living room . . . then the door slammed. Oh, God," she finished, covering her face with her hands, "I feel so stupid."

Todd pulled her hands from her face and draped an arm around her shoulders. "I can explain," he said as he led her down the hallway. "I left the front door open because I was out on the patio starting the grill and I was afraid I wouldn't hear the doorbell. And there isn't any furniture in the living room because I don't have any. And the door probably slammed as a result of the vacuum I created when I opened the back door and came back inside." He stopped in the kitchen and pulled her into his arms, kissing her tenderly. "And I don't think you're stupid at all. A little bit jumpy maybe, but not stupid."

She buried her face against his fleece-covered shoulder, laughing softly. "Not just a little bit. A whole lot jumpy."

"Calm enough now to make a salad?"

"Yes, but perhaps you shouldn't trust me with a knife

just yet. If you were to surprise me again, I might julienne *you* and add you to the salad."

"Fair warning." He backed away from her, pointedly protecting his back as he gestured in the direction of the refrigerator. "The salad makings are in the refrigerator. I'll check the steaks."

Glad to have something to do, Leandra opened the refrigerator door. A bottle of wine, a half-empty gallon of milk, and a tub of margarine sat on the top shelf. The remaining shelves were empty. *Evidently the man eats out a lot*, she thought with a smile. In the vegetable crisper she found a plastic bag of fresh vegetables, obviously purchased especially for their meal.

She carried the salad makings to the sink and began to wash them. Through the window she could see Todd leaning over the grill, smoke billowing around him in a white cloud that the wind caught and quickly chased away. Muscles rose and fell beneath the fabric of his sweatshirt as he turned the steaks. Something about the domestic scene they created spread a warm, satisfied glow through Leandra, bringing a half-smile to her lips as she sliced and chopped the vegetables for the salad.

Todd stuck his head in the back door. "Five minutes. Is the salad ready?"

"Just about. Where are your bowls?"

"In the cabinet to the left of the sink."

The back door closed as Leandra opened the cupboard. Two bowls, two plates, and an odd assortment of glasses were shoved onto one shelf. The other two were empty. So different from her own kitchen, filled as it was with dishes and pots and pans . . . and life. More so than the empty living room and the barren refrigerator, the contents of the cabinets pulled at her heartstrings, making her painfully aware of the loneliness of Todd's bachelor existence. Unexpected tears brimmed in her eyes.

Todd pushed through the back door, balancing a platter of steaks and grinning boyishly. A cold blast of air swept through the kitchen ahead of him. He stopped beside Leandra and touched his reddened nose to her cheek. "It's cold out there. How about a kiss to warm up the Galloping Gourmet?"

Leandra threw her arms around his neck and kissed him soundly, desperate to fill all the voids she saw in his life.

"I thought dessert was supposed to be after dinner," he mumbled against her lips. He pulled back slightly, grinning, but when he saw the tears glistening in Leandra's eyes, he set the platter on the counter beside him and turned back to her. He cupped her shoulders in his hands. "Hey, what's wrong?" he asked in concern.

Leandra shook her head and offered him a reassuring smile. "Nothing. I'm just glad to be here."

He pulled her into his arms and squeezed her tight against him. "Not half as glad as I am." He pressed his lips to her hair, then released her and picked up the platter of steaks. With an exaggerated bow, he gestured toward the table. "Your dinner, my lady."

Paris's most famed maitre d' couldn't have delivered the invitation with more aplomb. Matching his feigned air of formality, Leandra curtsied, then swept by him, giving him her most royal and haughty look. "Thank you, Galloping. You don't mind if I call you by your first name, do you?" she asked prudently. "After all, we will be sharing dinner."

Todd chuckled as he pulled out her chair. "Ah, the ice queen returneth."

"The ice queen?"

"That was my nickname for you at the Bachelor Auction." He scooted his own chair closer to the table, then added, "Of course, that was before I got to know you."

"The ice queen?" she repeated, her frown deepening as she cut into her steak. "I'm not sure I like that."

Todd fought back a smile. "Oh, but it fit you perfectly. You carried a sheet of ice around you thick enough to keep the Eskimos in igloos for years."

Leandra's fork clattered against her plate as she dropped it and looked at Todd in total disbelief. "Me? Are you sure you aren't thinking of someone else?"

"No." Todd took a healthy bite of steak and chewed on it, smiling all the while as he watched the expressions on Leandra's face change from disbelief, to shock, and finally to indignation. "You know what? You're cute when you're mad."

Leandra stabbed at a piece of steak. "I'm not mad."

"Yes, you are. When you're mad, you get this little twitch at the corner of your left eye and your lips thin until I can barely make out the little bow on your upper lip. Yep, you're mad all right," he said as he took another bite of his steak.

"I'm not mad, and I'm not an ice queen." Leandra snatched her napkin from her lap and crushed it beneath her hand on the table, eyeing Todd defiantly.

Her annoyance only fed his amusement. Laughing, he reared back in his chair, hooking his thumbs in the empty belt loops of his jeans. "I didn't say I *still* considered you the ice queen. But there are moments when the ice queen resurfaces."

"Todd Stillman, I think you are the most despicable man I have ever met."

He dropped his chair down on all four legs and leaned across the table, flashing his most charming smile. "And I think you are the most beautiful and desirable woman

I've ever met.'' He glanced at her plate, then back to her. "If you're through with your dinner, how about some dessert?''

Leandra's irritation melted under his gaze, and her bones turned to pliant clay. He had to be the most captivating and yet most aggravating man she'd ever known. Well, two can play this game, she thought impishly. She smiled sweetly as she, too, rested her elbows on the table and leaned across, placing scant inches between their noses. "Let's see. I believe dessert is to be bananas flambé. Right?''

Todd touched his mouth to hers, barely grazing her lips. "Unless you can think of something sweeter to dine on.''

His breath blew warm against her face, turning bones, which only moments ago had softened to clay, to jelly. Heat waves pulsed between them as Leandra inched closer for another kiss. A shrill ring rent the air, jerking them apart.

The phone rang a second time, but Todd didn't make a move to answer it. Puzzled, Leandra asked, "Aren't you going to see who it is?''

"Nope. I'm not on call. Now where were we?'' he asked as he leaned toward her again.

Worry lines creased Leandra's forehead. "But it could be Trey. I left your number with the babysitter.''

Todd sagged forward in defeat, then stretched behind him to snag the receiver from the wall unit behind him. "Dr. Stillman . . . I'm not on call. Dr. Fuller is . . . I see.'' He sighed deeply, then said, "Yes, I'll be there in a minute,'' before he stretched again to replace the phone.

"Damn!'' he muttered as he stood, tossing his napkin on the table. ''I've got to go to the hospital. They have an accident victim with chest injuries. Fuller is tied up in surgery, so I'll need to examine her.''

"Oh, Todd . . ."

He grabbed his jacket and shrugged it on as he stooped to kiss her. "Will you wait for me? I shouldn't be more than an hour or so."

Leandra laid her palm against his cheek as she raised her lips to meet his. She had been waiting for him for years. What difference would another hour or so make?

Todd pushed his way through the back door and glanced around the kitchen. The table had been cleared and the dishes washed. A solitary light glowed above the kitchen sink. *She's gone*, he thought wearily. He peeled off his coat and tossed it in the direction of the table. He missed and the jacket slid to the floor.

Bracing his hands on the edge of the sink, he dipped his head between his elbows. The hour or so he'd promised had turned into three. He knew he shouldn't have expected Leandra to wait, but he had. He lifted his head to the ceiling, his face a twisted mask of torment. God, how he needed her right now!

"Todd?"

He whirled at the sound of Leandra's voice and found her standing in the doorway. She stood with her arms hugged tight under her breasts, looking at him through sleep-swollen eyes. Her mascara was smeared, her hair was a tousled mess, and her feet were bare. Never had anyone looked better to him.

In three ground-eating steps, he crossed the room and crushed her to him, burying his cheek against her hair. He felt the faint beat of her pulse at her temple and squeezed her tighter in his arms until he felt the reassuring thud of her heart against his chest.

She sensed the desperation in his embrace. "Todd, what's wrong?" When he didn't answer, she gripped his forearms and pushed back to see his face. His eyes were filled with an anguish she couldn't begin to understand. She touched her hand to his cheek, and he covered it with his own trembling one.

"I thought you were gone. I—just let me hold you." He pulled her into his arms again and slowly rocked side to side, hugging her to him. Her warmth seeped into him, chasing away the chill that had penetrated him to the bone. Framing her face with his hands, he held her, staring deep into her eyes. "I need you."

Three words, simply said, but filled with a want, a sense of urgency Leandra could not deny. Something had happened to him while he'd been gone. Before he left, he'd been laughing and teasing her with innuendos. Now all signs of his earlier merriment were gone. He needed her. And for Leandra, that was enough.

In her eyes Todd found his answer, and he scooped her up into his arms and carried her to his bedroom. When he reached the bed, he gently laid her down, then sat down beside her, leaning his weight on his elbow as he brushed her hair away from her face.

"The patient I went to see at the hospital was a twenty-six-year-old woman. She was involved in an automobile accident and unfortunately had not put on her seat belt. On impact, her chest slammed against the steering wheel. To the naked eye, it looked like she had sustained only a simple contusion, but the emergency room staff detected muffled heart sounds. That's why they called me.

"When I inserted a needle into her pericardium and aspirated uncoagulated blood, I knew the sac around the heart had been damaged. We rushed her to the OR and opened her up to repair the ruptured sac. We worked for over two hours, but we couldn't save her. The damage was too extensive."

Tears filled Leandra's eyes as she listened. Todd brushed one from the corner of her eye, then moved his fingers to twine in the wisps of hair haloing her face on the pillow. "I deal with life and death every day, but when I looked at that young woman lying there, her life stolen from her by a stupid freak accident, I realized how fragile our lives and our time together are. All I could think about was getting back here to you." He heaved a shuddery sigh, never once moving his gaze from hers. "I needed to see you, touch you. I know that probably sounds crazy, doesn't it?"

Emotion formed a tight ball in Leandra's throat, stealing her voice. She could only shake her head in denial.

"When we were in Ixtapa, I told you I was a realist and wise enough to know few people ever find happiness in love." Todd brushed his lips across hers, then leaned back to look at her again, his fingertips still at her cheek.

"A part of me still believes that." Leandra opened her mouth to argue the point. Todd silenced her with a touch of his finger to her lips. "But there's another part of me that keeps hoping we'll be one of the few. I want to make love with you, Leandra, but I want you to understand what I'm offering. If it's not enough, say so now."

In his eyes she saw deep into the innermost recesses of his heart. Even though he couldn't voice it, she knew he loved her whether he was willing to admit it or not. She opened her arms to him and whispered, "It's enough."

He leaned into her embrace, molding his body to her slender frame. He squeezed his eyes shut and allowed his senses to fully absorb the pleasure of holding her, of feeling the reassuring cadence of her heartbeat against his chest. Gradually, the sense of melancholy he had borne since leaving the hospital faded.

Wanting to erase whatever of those emotions he had

transferred to her, he teased, "You know, I'm a little nervous about making love with a hopeless romantic."

"Really?"

He lifted his head and smiled down at her. "Yeah. I mean, what if I don't match up to your expectations?"

She met his smiling gaze and immediately knew his intentions. If possible, it made her love him all the more. She matched his lighthearted banter with her own. "Don't worry. Where you're concerned, I've learned not to have any."

He chuckled and pulled her into his arms again. Laughter was quickly replaced with desire as he felt each swell and valley of her body melt into his. Slowly, he worked his hands between their bodies to search out the buttons of her blouse. When the last one opened beneath his fingers, he slipped the blouse from her shoulders and moved his hands to her back, fumbling for the hook of her bra. Back and forth across the slender width of elastic he searched, but found nothing to unclasp.

Leandra's lips trembled against his as she tried not to laugh. Frustrated by his awkwardness, he sat up, frowning down at her. "What's so funny?"

"I'm sorry," she said, giving in to the laughter. "I don't mean to laugh. It's just that in all the movies and books, in the bedroom scenes, people's clothes seem to disappear like magic."

"Ah, yes. I forget you're the hopeless romantic. But I'm a realist. I *know* there has to be a way to remove that confounded contraption." He remained silent a moment, studying the situation thoughtfully. Without warning, he waved his arm in a wild arc over Leandra and yelled, "Abracadabra!"

Dubiously Leandra glanced down at her bra, then back up at him. "It didn't work."

"I noticed." He turned pleading eyes to her. "Give me a little hint."

"Front closure."

In the blink of an eye, he found the front clasp hidden by the soft lace and had the bra off, swinging it over his head before he tossed it to the floor. "Was that magic enough for you?"

"That depends."

"On what?"

"On what else you have up your sleeve, Mr. Magician."

Todd peeled his sweatshirt over his head, exposing a tempting amount of bare skin. He rolled his arms for her inspection. "As you can see, my little skeptic, I have nothing up my sleeve."

"How about your jeans?" she asked, arching one eyebrow at him suspiciously.

"Ah, yes, my jeans." He unsnapped them and pushed them down his thighs, then tumbled over onto his back beside her as he kicked them away. "I should have known you would guess. Only a true romantic would know where the magic is kept." Rolling to his side, he sought her lips with his and captured them, kissing her until she was breathless.

All signs of teasing were gone when Leandra raised her fevered gaze to his. "Show me some magic, Todd."

"With pleasure," he groaned huskily.

He rolled again until she was on top of him, and he quickly discarded the rest of her clothes until flesh met flesh. Passion skittered beneath fevered skin as they explored each other's bodies, their hands moving in a slow, tortuous journey, seeking the most pleasurable spots.

The magic he had promised was there, dazzling Leandra. His fingers were those of a sorcerer, touching here, trailing there, weaving a spell of wizardry around them.

In the silent room, her name, when whispered through his lips, became an incantation, entrancing her and binding her to him.

Blind to all but her need for him, she called to him, begging for release from this passionate bewitchment. He filled her, matching the rhythm he had already set thrumming within her until, together, they reached the zenith of the magical sphere they had created.

Todd lay flat on his back, staring thoughtfully at the ceiling. His hands were pillowed behind his head while one leg was hooked possessively across Leandra's thigh.

Jealous of the attention he was giving the ceiling, Leandra snuggled closer and smoothed her hand across the taut plane of his stomach. "What are you thinking?"

He glanced down at her. "Nothing really. Just daydreaming."

"A realist daydreaming?" She chuckled softly. "Surely you jest."

He snuggled her tighter against his side. "I'll bet a romantic like you has all kinds of dreams. Tell me some."

"I don't have any."

"Oh, come on."

"No, really I don't. When I was younger, I lived in a dream world, but not anymore."

"What changed?" Todd felt the butterfly movement of her smile against his chest.

"Everything. Fate seemed to decide the path of my life. Trey was the beginning."

For a moment, Todd was silent, thinking of how much of her youth was stolen by the responsibilities of single parenthood and wondering what dreams were stolen as well. He dipped his head to look at her again. "What were your dreams?"

Leandra glanced away, embarrassed. "You'll laugh."

Quickly, Todd crossed his heart. "No, I won't. Promise."

"To be a housewife and a mother."

He tossed back his head and roared with laughter. He knew he had promised, but he couldn't help himself. He laughed even harder, his ribs merrily bouncing against Leandra's cheek.

When he felt her tense against him, he lifted his head off the pillow to better see her face and saw the flush of anger warming her cheeks. "You're serious, aren't you?" he asked incredulously.

"Yes."

A *housewife?* It was unbelievable! Most teenaged girls dreamed of being movie stars and models and jet-setting around the world. Leandra had dreamed of being a housewife—and meant it.

He turned onto his side, propping his weight on his elbow and his head on his open palm, totally fascinated. "You mean you'd rather be home, cooking and cleaning and changing diapers than be some famous model or some hotshot executive?"

Leandra gathered the covers defensively about her. "Yes. Is that so hard to believe?"

"Well, yeah, it is." He saw the hurt look his comment brought to her eyes and sought to erase it by adding, "Commendable, but rare."

"Great." Leandra twisted away from him, tugging the covers all the way to her chin. "First the ice queen, and now I suppose you'll nickname me Susie Homemaker or—"

"Precious or Darling," he finished for her. He chuckled when she continued to eye him defiantly. "If your dream was to be a housewife, I think that's wonderful." He tipped her chin up higher and smiled down at her. "I'd still think it wonderful if your dream was to be an astronaut."

The tension slowly eased out of Leandra. "You're a pain, you know it?"

He laughed and hugged her to him. "I know, but my magical abilities make up for it."

Oh, yes, his magical abilities more than compensated for his teasing, she thought with a sigh. But she liked his teasing, too. He brought laughter and sunshine into her life—as her son did, yet differently.

They lay for a moment, content in each other's arms. Leandra knew it was late but was reluctant to end their time together. She smoothed her hands from Todd's shoulder, down the length of his arm, to the watch on his wrist. The illumined dial revealed to her the time, and she groaned as she slowly sat up. "I've got to go. My babysitter will never forgive me for staying out so late."

Todd caught her hand before she could rise. "Couldn't you just call or something?"

Leandra laughed at the absurdity of his suggestion. "No, I couldn't *call or something*. Remember? I'm a mother, and I have responsibilities to my son. Besides, I have to work in the morning, and so do you." She moved about the room, picking up her discarded clothes, then slipped into the adjoining bath to dress. When she returned to the bedroom, Todd was sitting on the bed, resting his arms on the sheet steepled over his bent knees.

He watched her movements as she combed her fingers through her rumpled hair. She was leaving, and he hated the thought. "When will I see you again?"

"What's your schedule like?"

His shoulders sagged. "Packed. I have this *thing* I have to attend Friday night." His eyes brightened. "Why don't you go with me? It'll be the only way I can survive the boredom."

Leandra laughed at his desperate expression. "Sorry. I've already made plans for Friday night. But Saturday's good." She leaned over the bed and pressed her lips to his, the flavor of their lovemaking still fresh on his lips. "Now come on, I have to go home."

"I think I'm in love."

Ellen wheeled from the stove, the spoon she held dripping chocolate fudge onto the kitchen's bricked floor while she stared wide-eyed at Todd's grinning face. "What did you say?"

"I said I think I'm in love."

"My heavens!" She dropped the spoon back into the saucepan and switched off the burner. Using the skirt of her apron, she quickly wiped her hands as she crossed the room. She dropped onto the kitchen chair opposite Todd's. "I can't believe my little brother is saying this. So who's the lucky girl?"

"Leandra Gallagher."

"What! But I thought—"

"I know. I know. But she isn't at all like what we thought. She's beautiful."

"*We* thought! You mean *you* thought. And as I recall, you never once questioned her looks. It was her character you doubted."

"I was wrong. She's wonderful. Kind and loving. And a fantastic mother."

"Mother! She has children?"

"One. A boy. He broke his arm while we were in Mexico. Leandra was so upset." Todd chuckled. "At first I thought she was going to insist on coming home, but after I called Sidney Greenwold—he set the boy's arm—

and confirmed the boy was fine, she agreed to stay. Leandra's mother was there with Trey, and she assured us everything was—''

A beeping sound interrupted Todd. He listened to his pager's garbled message, then stood. ''Sorry, Sis. I've got to get back to the hospital.''

''But, Todd—''

''Later. Okay?'' Todd bent and pecked his sister's cheek before disappearing out the back door.

Ellen continued to sit at the table long after Todd had gone, still shocked by her brother's announcement.

''Ellen?''

''In here,'' she called to her husband as she stood and walked slowly to the stove. She turned the burner back on under the saucepan and began to stir, trying to salvage the lumpy fudge.

''Todd gone?''

''Yes, the hospital paged him.'' Frowning at the thick blobs of chocolate, Ellen picked up the saucepan and dropped it into the sink. Then, taking her husband by the arm, she guided him to a chair. ''You'd better sit down, Wes. You aren't going to believe this.''

She sank down in the chair Todd had vacated only a short time before. ''Todd is in love with Leandra Gallagher.''

''You're kidding!''

''No, he told me so himself.'' Her eyes took on a dreamy cast. ''Todd finally in love. I honestly thought it would never happen. Isn't it wonderful, Wes?''

''Yes, I suppose so.''

Ellen's jaw sagged. ''Wes! This is Todd we're talking about. The world's most determined bachelor. Why aren't you excited for him?''

''I am.''

"Well, you could've fooled me."

"It's just that I discovered something last week about Leandra."

"What?"

"She has a child."

"Is that all?" Ellen laughed. "Todd already knows that. The boy broke his arm while Leandra and Todd were in Mexico and—"

Wes placed a restraining hand on Ellen's arm. "Do you remember Friday when I took one of my students to the hospital after an accident on the playground?"

Puzzled, Ellen replied, "Yes, I remember."

"That boy was Leandra's son."

"What a fluke!"

"Yes, it was. At the hospital I met Leandra's mother. Inadvertently, I referred to the boy's parents—in the plural sense. Mrs. Gallagher was quick to inform me that Trey doesn't have a father. He's illegitimate."

Ellen jumped up from the table, her hands planted in tight fists at her hips. "Wesley Jansen! I'm surprised at you. The legitimacy of Leandra Gallagher's son wouldn't change Todd's opinion of her."

"It might." Wesley stood and moved to his wife, cupping her elbows in his hands as he looked into her eyes. "When I went back to school to fill out the reports, I looked at the copy of Trey's birth certificate in his file."

Ellen tensed in his arms.

"Robert Todd Stillman is listed as the boy's father."

Ellen's hands flew to her mouth, her face stricken as she stared at Wes. "Todd's son? Oh, my God! Why didn't he tell me?"

Wesley tightened his grip on Ellen's elbows. "Because the boy's not Todd's son. Trey's your father's child."

"Daddy's! But that would make him . . . Oh, my

God!'' She dropped into a chair and stared numbly at the opposite wall. After a moment, she lifted her pain-filled gaze to her husband. ''Wes, we've got to tell Todd.''

''No, Ellen. It's not our place to tell him. Leandra must be the one to do that.''

# SEVEN

Mink-draped shoulders brushed black tuxedo sleeves as guests wound their way through the colorful displays of prominent Southwest artists. Other guests stood in scattered groups, laughing and talking while sipping bubbly champagne. Members of the hospital auxiliary moved through the crowd to place discreet sold signs on the pieces of art purchased at the charity event.

Dressed in his penguin suit, Todd stood in a corner of the room hungrily eyeing the hors d'oeuvres table. He'd missed dinner because of an emergency at the hospital, and lunch had been so long ago he couldn't remember what he'd eaten. Intent on reaching the table before it was picked clean, he began to weave his way across the room.

"Todd! Glad you could make it, son."

Todd stopped and shook the hand extended to him by the robust gray-haired man. "It's good to see you, Mr. Greeley."

"You remember my wife."

Smiling, Todd shook her hand as well. "Yes, though it's been awhile."

"And my niece, Vanessa."

Todd turned to the buxom redhead beside Mrs. Greeley. "No, I don't believe I've had the pleasure."

Smiling coyly, Vanessa slipped her hand into his. "I was beginning to think I was the only person here under the age of fifty. It's nice to see that I'm not."

Todd eased his hand from hers. "I'm sure there are others."

"I wish you'd look at that!"

Surprised at the venomous tone in Mrs. Greeley's voice, Todd turned to her, then followed her angry gaze, which was centered on the front door.

Todd's heart swelled at the sight that greeted him. Leandra, dressed in a red sequined gown, stood in the doorway, talking with the president of the hospital board. Diamonds, rivaling the glittering radiance of her dress, dangled from her ears. Draped casually over one shoulder was a mahogany mink stole.

"Shameless, she is. Parading around in Mamie's mink like that. The absolute nerve of her!"

Todd frowned. *Who the hell is Mamie,* he wondered, *and why would Leandra wear the woman's mink?* He shrugged off the thought while the pleasure of seeing her again drew a smile to his face.

"Living in sin they are, and right there in Mamie's house."

It took a moment for Mrs. Greeley's words to register. Living in sin? Todd watched in sick fascination as Leandra turned and slipped her arm through the crook of the gentleman's arm beside her. With her elbow tucked securely at the side of the white-haired man, she scanned the room, her eyes widening in surprise when they met Todd's gaze.

Suddenly, Todd felt as if the room were closing in on him. There wasn't enough air to breathe. How could she do this to him? Two nights ago, they had become lovers. And now . . . With one last damning look, Todd turned his back on her. After offering a hasty apology to the Greeleys, he stalked toward a side exit.

When the door closed behind him, Todd fell back against it, squeezing his eyes shut and slamming his fists against the steel panel. "Damn her!" he muttered through clenched teeth as he pushed away from the door. Obviously, her attraction for older men hadn't ended with his father. Leandra Gallagher had found herself another sugar daddy—one older and apparently more generous than the senior Robert Todd Stillman, but a sugar daddy nonetheless.

Leandra felt nauseous. The condemning look Todd had leveled at her before he disappeared in the crowded room had left her feeling weak and confused. He couldn't be angry because she was there. She'd told him she already had plans for the evening.

If not for John, she'd leave the silly charity function right now and go home. The evening was ruined for her. But she couldn't ask John to leave. He'd looked forward to the evening out for weeks.

Needing a private moment to regain her composure, she whispered to John, "If you'll excuse me, I'm going to see if I can find the ladies' room."

She crossed the room and pushed through the door to the ladies' lounge. Dropping down onto one of the wicker chairs, she covered her face with her hands and willed the tears that burned her eyes to recede.

From the adjoining room, voices drifted out to Leandra. Her own name reached her ear, and puzzled, she straightened, straining to hear the conversation.

"If you ask me, John Warner is a doddering old fool.

Cavorting around with a girl half his age. Poor Mamie, lying sick in that house all those years while they carried on right beneath her very nose.''

Anger rose in Leandra's throat, nearly choking her. She'd heard similar comments before, but it didn't make the vicious gossip any easier to swallow. No one understood her relationship with John Warner, nor did they bother to ask. They only assumed.

"Now that she's dead, the girl's even taken to wearing Mamie's clothes. Someone ought to do something."

A second voice asked, "Like what?"

"I don't know. Maybe they ought to commit John. He's acting crazy enough. Believe me, I know. Why, just the other day I saw him with that child of hers. . . ."

Leandra had heard enough. She ran from the room, wanting nothing but to escape the sound of the women's malicious voices. With her head bent to hide her tears, she rounded a corner and flattened herself against the wall of a tuxedoed chest.

Without looking up, she mumbled an apology and brushed past the man.

His hand caught her arm, jerking her to a stop at his side. Surprised, Leandra lifted tear-filled eyes and met the hostile gaze of Todd Stillman. In his eyes she saw the same contempt she'd heard in the women's muffled voices in the lounge.

"Let go of me," she whispered fiercely as she pulled free and rushed past him. At the door, she hurriedly left John a message, telling him she'd gone home, then ran from the stifling room.

"Leandra! Wait!" Todd's voice called from behind her.

She quickened her pace, hurrying to the valet stand. "I need a taxi, please."

"I'll take you home." Todd caught her elbow in his

strong grasp and firmly led her away from the curious eyes of the parking attendants.

When they were out of earshot, Leandra jerked free of him. "I thought you left."

"I did. I came back to talk to you." He opened the passenger door. "Get in."

Stubbornly, Leandra folded her arms across her heaving chest. "No."

With a stern look, Todd ordered, "I said get in. If necessary, I'll pick you up and put you there."

He would, too. She could tell by the determined gleam in his eye. Leandra's pent-up breath whooshed angrily out of her, forming a vaporous cloud in the cool night air. Jerking her skirt's long tail clear of the door, she sat down hard on the leather seat and slammed the door behind her.

A moment later Todd's door opened, then slammed shut. Silence screamed within the car's interior for ten long tedious seconds before Todd demanded in a tight voice, "I want to know who he is."

"*He* who?"

"The man you were with."

Leandra pulled her stole protectively around her. "*He* is none of your business."

Todd's fist hit the steering wheel, making Leandra jump. "Dammit, Leandra. He *is* my business. I want to know who he is and what he means to you."

"And just exactly what makes it your business, Todd Stillman?"

"Because I care about you, that's what!"

Leandra sucked in a shocked breath and held it until her lungs burned. She stared at his shadowy profile in the darkness, afraid to trust what she'd heard. "You what?"

"You heard me. Now who is he?"

"John Warner."

"And . . ."

"And I live with him."

"Damn!" Todd hit the steering wheel again with a balled fist. "Why, Leandra? Tell me why!"

"My parents arranged it. They—"

"Your parents! Oh, my God!"

Leandra placed a restraining hand on his arm. Through the jacket of his tuxedo she felt the strength of his anger but realized the anger was directed not *at* her but *for* her. The knowledge that he cared enough to fight for her opened up her heart and allowed the love she'd kept locked away to spill out. The time had come to open the box of tightly guarded secrets and reveal them to Todd. "Please. It's all so complicated. If you'll just listen, I think you'll understand."

She took a long, steadying breath. "I was seventeen when I discovered I was pregnant with Trey. To save me the embarrassment my pregnancy would have caused in the small town where we lived, my parents arranged for me to come to Oklahoma City to live with John Warner. Daddy worked for John and knows him well, and it was agreed that I would live with the Warners until the baby was born. In exchange for room and board, I was to be a companion for Mamie, John's wife. Mamie was ill and virtually bedridden when I first came to live with them.

"It was understood from the beginning that after the baby came I would put him up for adoption and return home to Tecumseh. But with each passing month, the baby became more and more a part of me. I finally realized I couldn't give him up."

Her lips trembled as she turned her head to stare unseeing out the passenger window. "I think Mamie realized I couldn't go through with it even before I did. During the months before Trey's birth, Mamie's health seemed to improve. She taught me to knit. We made booties and blankets and talked about names for the baby."

Her voice drifted off. After a moment, she shook her head to clear her thoughts and continued. "When Trey was born, John and Mamie came to the hospital to see Trey and me. They asked me to stay with them. Trey was like a gift to them, the child they'd never been able to have."

The memories were hard for Leandra. She swiped at a stray tear. "I accepted their offer. Just after Trey's fourth birthday, Mamie died." Leandra turned to Todd, her face ravaged by the painful memory. "I couldn't leave John then. Trey and I had become so much a part of his life. I couldn't leave, yet I couldn't stay either. Since I didn't have Mamie to care for anymore, I didn't feel it was fair to accept room and board. John already had a house-keeper, so that option was out. Then he offered me a job in his office." Leandra lifted her hands in a helpless shrug. "It seemed the perfect solution."

Shame ripped through Todd. He had allowed his opin-ion of Leandra to be twisted by the malicious gossip he'd heard. He hated himself for distrusting her and even more for the unanswered questions that continued to plague him, but he had to ask, to put all the demons that haunted him to rest. "What about all the jewelry and the mink? Did John give those to you?"

Leandra's answering laugh sounded hollow in the close confines of the car. "I see you heard the rumors, too." She fingered the diamonds dangling from her ears. "No. John didn't give me these. They were Mamie's. Since she didn't have any children of her own, I guess I became like a daughter to her—or at the least a favorite niece. She knew how much I loved beautiful things. In her will, she bequeathed all her jewelry and furs to me." Leandra glanced at Todd. "She also gave me her mother's antique bedroom furniture.'' She shook her head sadly as she dipped her head, to stare unseeing at the hands she clasped tightly in her lap. ''I guess people would hold that against me, too, if they knew.''

In the distance, an ambulance raced by, its siren wailing.

''I'm sorry, Leandra.''

''Don't be. I'm used to it.''

''No, I mean for not trusting you, for not believing in you.'' His fingers sought hers in the darkness. ''Forgive me. Please.''

*Coward!* Leandra silently accused herself as she paced across her bedroom. The opportunity had been there. All she had to do was blurt it out. She could have told Todd everything and been done with it. But no! When he'd taken her hand and looked at her with that woeful expression, she'd stopped just short of the whole truth. She'd held back that one slim particle of information about her past—the one fact he deserved to know, the one fact that could possibly send him running.

She flopped down on her bed and yanked a tissue from the box on the nightstand. *A sniveling coward, that's what I am,* she thought as she wiped the dampness from her cheeks, then blew her nose. She'd told Todd everything about her past—except that he was the father of her child.

A soft knock at her bedroom door had her grabbing a fresh tissue and blotting at her eyes. ''Yes?''

''Leandra? Can I come in?''

The concern in John's voice created new waves of guilt in Leandra. Submerged in her own overwhelming problem, she'd forgotten all about him. She hurried to the door and flung it open. ''Oh, John. I'm sorry. I hope you didn't leave the party on my account. I wasn't feeling well and—''

"Don't try to pull the wool over my eyes, young lady." John took her by the elbow and firmly guided her to the chaise lounge, then sat down beside her. "Something's bothering you and has been for weeks. I think it's time you and I had a talk."

Moisture pooled in Leandra's eyes. "It's nothing really. It's just that . . ."

"Come on, Leandra. Out with it."

Leandra's lower lip quivered, and she bit down on it, trying to stem the flood of tears threatening to overflow.

"Does it have something to do with the man I saw you with at the party?"

Leandra could only nod.

"Is he the one you went to Mexico with?"

Tears streamed down her face. "Yes," she managed to choke out.

John jumped up, his face tight in anger. "If that man has hurt you, by God, I'll—"

Leandra caught his sleeve. "No, it's not that. It's . . . Oh, John. He's Trey's father."

John's bushy eyebrows lifted in a high inverted V. "He's who?"

"He's Trey's father." Leandra dropped her hand to her lap, her shoulders drooping beneath the weight of her confession.

Catching the crease of his slacks just above his knees, John hitched them up as he slowly sank down beside Leandra. "Well, well, well. Who is he?"

"Todd Stillman."

Silence stretched between them for a moment before John spoke again, his voice gruff. "Does this mean you'll be moving out?"

Immediately, Leandra grabbed for his hand and squeezed it reassuringly. "Oh, no, John. I could never leave you.

And besides," she said miserably, "when Todd finds out about Trey, I'll probably never see him again."

"You mean to tell me this Stillman fellow doesn't even know about the boy?"

"No. I never told him."

"Why not?"

"I tried. When I first discovered I was pregnant, I came to Oklahoma City to see him, but he'd already left for medical school. I talked to his father instead."

"And?"

"And his father let me know in no uncertain terms that his son would *not* be held responsible for any bastard child. When I insisted the baby was Todd's, Mr. Stillman wrote me out a check for five thousand dollars and told me to get lost. I didn't want the money. I wanted Todd. But his father refused to tell me where he'd gone. I called the registrar's office at the University of Oklahoma, and all they could tell me was that Todd had graduated in May and was not currently registered. I didn't know where else to look."

John's face flushed an angry red. "I wish I'd known. By God, I'd have slapped a paternity suit on them so fast the old buzzard wouldn't have known what hit him."

Leandra couldn't help smiling at John's big talk. "Thanks. But it's best things worked out as they did. I didn't really know Todd—"

"Now wait just a minute, young lady. I may be old, but I'm not senile yet. You obviously *knew* him or you wouldn't have been carrying his child."

Leandra felt a blush warm her cheeks. Eight years later, she still couldn't draw a reasonable explanation to that statement herself. Raised in a strict, moral home, she couldn't believe she'd made love with a man she'd only known for a few short hours.

"It sounds crazy, I know, but I really didn't know him. We met at a fraternity party on Lake Thunderbird. I went to the party with a girlfriend. She was dating one of the guys at the time. It was kind of a wild party. A lot of drinking. Todd was there. He was alone and kept pretty much to himself."

Leandra paused and wrapped the tissue around her fingers as the memory enveloped her. "There was something about him . . . something almost sad. I didn't know anyone at the party other than my girlfriend, so I started talking to him. After a while, the noise level made it difficult to hear, and he asked me to go for a walk."

Leandra turned to John. "I realize it's hard to believe, but I fell in love with him in a matter of hours. I'd have done anything he asked of me." She ducked her head, embarrassed as she realized the irony of her admission. After a moment, she lifted her head and stared out her bedroom window to the darkness beyond. "I used to dream he would somehow find out about Trey and me and come back for us. Unfortunately, he never did. I didn't see him again until his picture appeared in the paper a couple of weeks ago."

"Do you mean to tell me you went to that Bachelor Auction knowing he would be there?"

"Yes."

"Why, for God's sake?"

"Revenge. I wanted to hurt him. To get even for all the pain he'd caused me." Leandra tossed back her head and laughed, but the sound lacked humor. "Unfortunately, my plan backfired. Todd didn't even remember me. And judging from something he said while we were in Mexico, he was too drunk the night I got pregnant to even remember what he did."

"So now what are you going to do?"

"I don't know," she replied wearily. "I just don't know."

John arrived at his office the next morning, feeling the weight of every one of his sixty-six years. After a sleepless night, he'd left the house early, purposely avoiding an encounter with Leandra. He knew what he had to do, but knowing didn't make it any easier. He buried himself in a pile of paperwork, but at nine o'clock he threw down his pen and pressed the button for his secretary.

"Yes, Mr. Warner?"

"Tell Leandra I want to see her in my office."

"When?"

"Now!" John roared impatiently.

Minutes later Leandra peeked around his office door. "Did you want to see me, John?"

"Yes." He gestured toward the leather chair facing his desk without ever looking at her, then snapped, "Sit down!" when she hesitated a moment too long in the doorway. He turned his attention back to the pile of papers lying on his desk.

Although well accustomed to his gruffness, Leandra felt a flicker of uneasiness. He'd never talked to her this way before. "Is something wrong?"

Ignoring her question, John scrawled his name across the bottom of a page, tossed it to the side, and picked up another letter from the pile.

"I want you out of my house."

Leandra stared, sure she had misunderstood him. "What did you say?"

"I want you out of my house. I'm going to Phoenix to visit Mamie's sister for a couple of weeks. When I get back, I expect you to be gone." He pushed a sealed envelope across the desk toward her. "Here's your paycheck.

It includes two weeks' severance pay. Clean out your desk, and give your keys to my secretary.''

A kick in the jaw couldn't have stunned Leandra more. ''But, John . . . why?''

''Just take your check and go.''

For a moment, Leandra sat and stared at him in disbelief. Eight years she had lived with John Warner. She'd heard rumors of his ruthlessness but she had never been touched by his anger before. Why was he doing this to her? What had she done to anger him so? She searched her mind for a reason but found nothing to explain his actions. Unless . . . unless it was what she'd told him the night before.

John raised his head and glared at her. ''I said go!''

Leandra flinched at the barked command. She stood and pulled the envelope from the desk. ''I'm sorry, John,'' she said softly, then turned and walked slowly from his office.

Leandra willed herself not to cry. The sympathetic looks her co-workers sent her as she emptied her desk made it difficult. Within twenty minutes, her personal belongings were boxed and the keys to her desk returned to Marge Harris, John's secretary.

Marge had worked for John for over twenty years and was privy to his personal life. Unlike the others at the office, she knew the circumstances behind Leandra's presence in John's home. It was a secret she guarded as tightly as she did her own love for John Warner. She accepted the keys from Leandra but caught Leandra's hand in her own for a moment.

''I don't know what's gotten into him, Leandra, but he loves you. You know that. You're like a daughter to him.''

Marge's words tugged at Leandra's carefully controlled emotions. Tears welled in her eyes, and she fought them back. She wouldn't cry . . . not yet anyway. Stealing a last glance at John's closed office door, she picked up her box and hurried from the office.

When she reached her car, she sagged against the steering wheel and let the tears fall. What would she do? Where would she go? Todd's name formed on her trembling lips. He would know what to do. He would help her. As quickly as the thought formed, she discarded it. The problem was hers, not his. She would work it out on her own.

"But why do we have to move, Mom?" Trey asked.

Leandra took the stuffed animal Trey held and jammed it into the box, closing the cardboard flaps before they could pop open again. Struggling to stretch masking tape across the lid, she calmly replied, "Because Papa John wants us to."

"Doesn't Papa John love us anymore?"

Seeing the confusion in her son's face, Leandra stood and wrapped her arms around him, hugging him hard against her breast. "Yes, he loves us. He just needs a little privacy that's all."

"Will he come and visit us?"

Leandra squeezed her eyes shut, blocking out her own pain. She had to be strong for Trey. John was like a grandfather to him, and this house was the only one he'd ever known. Leaving them both would be hard on Trey, and Leandra intended to make the separation as easy as possible on her son. "Sure he will, as soon as we're settled." She silently prayed her promise wasn't a lie. Holding Trey out at arm's length, she said, "Now why don't you sit down and tell me about your day at school while I finish up here."

Trey climbed up on the bare mattress and pulled his legs under him Indian style. "I made an A on my spelling test, and Mrs. Gruber gave me a star."

"Great! How about your math? Did you turn in your homework?"

"Yeah." He reached for his backpack and dug around in the mass of wrinkled papers, his search for the returned assignment awkward because of his cumbersome cast. A small yellow envelope fell to the floor beside Leandra.

"What's this?"

"An invitation to Robby Jansen's birthday party."

"Who is Robby Jansen?"

"A kid in my class. His dad's the principal. Neat, huh?"

Leandra frowned. "What's neat?"

"Having your dad for principal."

Leandra laughed as she stood, a load of books stacked high in her arms. "Yeah, that's pretty neat."

Trey was thoughtful for a moment. "What does my dad do?"

Shocked by the unexpected question, Leandra lost her grip on the books and they crashed to the floor. She quickly stooped to pick them up. "He's a doctor," she said, carefully avoiding her son's gaze.

"How come I've never seen him?"

Leandra sank back on her heels. Trey had not asked about his father in years. She had known that at some point he'd become curious and she'd have to explain everything to him, but at the moment she had more than enough to deal with. She certainly didn't need the added complication of trying to explain his father's absence to him. "Why are you asking all these questions?"

Trey shrugged. "Just wondered." He traced the stripe on the mattress ticking with a stubby finger sticking out of the end of the plaster cast. "Bryan Johnson's dad doesn't live with him, but Bryan gets to visit his dad one weekend every month."

Leandra moved to sit beside Trey. "Bryan's parents are divorced, and they agreed to share custody of Bryan. That means he gets to live with both of them."

"Why didn't you agree to share cus—cus—"

"Custody."

"—custody of me?"

Leandra took a deep breath and slowly blew it out, bargaining for time. How could she explain the circumstances of his birth to her seven-year-old son—a little boy who thought a man and woman had to be married to have babies? "Before you were ever born, your father moved far away. It was decided that you should always live with me."

"Oh." Trey absorbed that bit of information, then glanced up at Leandra. "Can I have a cookie?"

Leandra breathed a sigh of relief as she silently thanked God for the short attention span of the seven-year-old mind. She hugged Trey to her. "Yes, you may have a cookie. Tell Mrs. Brumbelow I said it was okay."

# EIGHT

Leandra moved like an automaton through the next two weeks. She found an apartment near Trey's school and moved what few personal effects she had from John's home. Her possessions were easy enough to transfer. Trey's bedroom furniture, toys, and clothes and her own clothing. A pitiful accumulation after eight years.

After dropping Trey off at school each day, Leandra spent the mornings scouring used furniture stores and junk shops, looking for furniture and accessories to fill the empty living room and dinette of their small apartment. It was a big change from the spaciousness and luxury of John Warner's home, but the apartment was home now and Leandra was determined to make it as comfortable as possible.

In the afternoons, she studied the want ads. She needed a job and fast. A careful study of her finances had indicated she could live approximately six months on what money she had managed to save over the years. But in January—two short months away—Trey's second semester tuition would be due. She could take him out of the expensive private school John had insisted upon financing, but that would mean one more major change for Trey to adapt to.

*Now what do I do?* Leandra thought miserably as she sat in the carpool line, waiting for Trey to come out of the school building. She'd just completed an interview for a secretarial job with a local law firm and had been turned down. No letter of recommendation from her last employer and not enough education, they'd said. It was the same response she'd received from all the other would-be employers she'd applied to. Without a high school degree, it seemed the only job available to her was that of a waitress.

But she couldn't take that job either. The hours were wrong. It would mean working at night, and she couldn't leave Trey alone with no one to watch him.

Trey emerged from the crowd of students pouring out of the school building and headed toward her car.

"Hi, Mom!"

"Hi, yourself. How was school?"

"Super. Do you have Robby's present?"

Leandra waved a hand in the direction of the back seat. "Back there. Wrapped and ready. The invitation is in my purse. Why don't you read me the address again to refresh my memory?"

The address Trey read was only a few blocks from John's home. As she drove through the residential section of Nichols Hills, out of the corner of her eye, Leandra watched Trey's head turn as they passed John's street. Two weeks and not a word from the man who had been so much a part of their lives. Trey hadn't said anything, but Leandra knew he missed his Papa John. She worried about how much pain her son was suppressing.

"There it is, Mom. The house with balloons on the mailbox."

"So it is." Leandra parked at the curb in front of the Jansens' home, then reached in the back seat for the brightly wrapped package. With forced gaiety, she challenged, "Race you to the door."

They reached the front porch simultaneously. Trey pushed the doorbell while Leandra smoothed a hand through his hair. "Now mind your manners, and don't be too rambunctious. You have to be careful of that arm."

"Oh, Mom." Trey ducked from beneath her hand just as the door opened.

"Hi, I'm Ellen, Robby's mom." The woman in the doorway knelt down in front of Trey. "And you must be Trey Gallagher." She touched a hand to the cleft in his chin, studying him a moment while a smile slowly spread across her face. "I should have guessed."

*Guessed what?* Leandra wondered in confusion. The thought of leaving Trey in this strange woman's care was beginning to concern her.

Before Leandra could act on her fear, Ellen stood and guided Trey through the door. "All the kids are in the game room playing video games. Why don't you join them?" Then she turned to Leandra. "And you must be Leandra. We meet at last. I've heard so much about you."

Puzzled as to how the woman could have heard about her, Leandra asked, "You have?"

"Yes! And I'm anxious to see if it's all true." Ellen motioned for Leandra to follow her. "Come in and have a cup of coffee with me while I finish decorating the cake."

"If you're sure I won't be in the way."

"Heavens, no. I'm always running late." The woman chatted away as if they were old friends, confusing Leandra even further. She didn't know Ellen Jansen, so how could the woman know so much about her?

*Ellen Jansen!* Suddenly the name registered. The woman from the auction who had called to arrange the television taping. Embarrassment warmed Leandra's cheeks as she remembered how rude she'd been to the woman. Then why on earth was Ellen being so nice? And whom had she talked to about Leandra?

As they moved through the formal living and dining rooms, Leandra's baffled thoughts fled, stolen by the splendor of the rooms. Emerald green walls served as a dramatic background for exquisite antiques and Oriental accessories. The rooms were eclectic in style, holding a delightful mixture of antique and contemporary furnishings that matched the personality of the woman who led Leandra through them.

"Your home is gorgeous," Leandra said, her voice filled with undisguised surprise.

Ellen glanced back over her shoulder as she pushed through the kitchen's swinging door. "That statement is usually followed by, 'How do you do it on a principal's salary?' "

Embarrassed at hearing her very thoughts verbalized, Leandra hastened to explain, "Oh, please . . . I didn't mean to imply—"

Ellen laughed again. "It's okay. Our home always shocks people. And no, we don't manage all this," she said with a careless wave of her hand, "on Wesley's salary." She stepped to the center island and picked up the pastry bag of icing, then gestured with it toward a bar stool. "Have a seat. The coffee's on the bar. Help yourself."

Bewildered by the woman's friendliness and blunt honesty, Leandra complied.

"This house belonged to my parents. When they divorced, they gave it to Wesley and me." Ellen paused to lick some blue icing from her finger. "Most of the furnishings and knickknacks around we've picked up over the years at estate auctions. That's our hobby—attending estate auctions. Plus, we have several oil leases that my dad gave us for birthdays and Christmas and the like. As a result," she laughed good-naturedly as she squeezed a fine line of icing around the cake's edge, "we live fairly well on a principal's salary." She paused, eyeing the cake critically. "What do you think?"

"Looks great to me."

"Good." Ellen dropped the pastry bag on the counter and picked up a dish towel to wipe her hands. "Now tell me where you got that dress."

Evidently, Ellen's thoughts flashed as quickly as her smile. Leandra glanced down at her sweatshirt dress. "I made it. Not the dress," she corrected. "I bought that at a discount store, but I painted the design."

Ellen raised an arched brow, obviously impressed. "You're good. Do you sell them?"

Leandra laughed. "Heavens, no! It's just a hobby."

Ellen's mouth formed a pout. "Darn. I'd love to have one."

"I'd be happy to—"

"Anybody home?" a muffled voice called from the front of the house.

"We're in the kitchen. Come on back."

The swinging door opened, and Todd stepped through, smiling happily. "Where's the birthday boy? I brought—" He stopped when he saw Leandra, his smile melting into a frown. "What are you doing here?"

"I brought Trey to Robby's birthday party. What are *you* doing here?"

He lifted the gift he held in his hand. "I came for the party."

Ellen looked from one to the other, then focused on Leandra's puzzled face. "You mean you didn't know? Todd's my brother."

"No, I didn't know."

Todd shrugged. "Now you do." He swirled a finger around the bowl of icing and stuck it in his mouth, sucking noisily. "Umm—mmm. Good stuff. When do we cut the cake, Sis?"

Ellen swatted his hand as he hungrily eyed the decorated cake. "Later. Why don't you entertain Leandra while I go check on the boys?" She paused in the doorway, arching one eyebrow meaningfully at Leandra. "And you make sure he stays out of the cake."

With that last directive, Ellen disappeared behind the swinging door.

Uneasy without Ellen's vivacious presence to act as a buffer between her and Todd, Leandra sipped at her now tepid coffee.

"I've been trying to get ahold of you for weeks. The housekeeper said you'd moved but wouldn't give me your telephone number or address."

"Mrs. Brumbelow is rather protective."

"So I gathered." He pulled up a bar stool and sat down beside her. "You could have let me know you were moving."

*Yes, she could have*, she thought guiltily, *but she hadn't*. The truth was, she hadn't allowed herself to call him. It would have been too easy to accept the help she suspected he would have offered. And besides, with all she had needed to deal with in the last three weeks, Todd had been the easiest problem to put on the back burner.

Unable to meet his gaze, Leandra stared into her half-empty cup. "I haven't had the chance. I found an apartment on Britton Road, not far from Trey's school, and I've been busy settling us in and looking for a job."

"I thought you worked for John?"

"I did."

"What happened?"

"He fired me."

"Why?"

Leandra didn't have an answer to that question, only her suppositions, and they—like all her problems, past and present—came full circle, leading her back to Todd. The stressful weeks of worrying about where she and Trey would live, and how they would manage financially, compounded by her own guilt at not having told Todd the whole truth weighed heavily on her.

She could handle her responsibilities as a parent. She was young and strong and had always managed to take care of herself and Trey. But the burden of her past and the secrets surrounding it were too much to carry anymore. She wanted to be free, and freedom would come only when she'd admitted it all.

"Todd, I need to talk to you."

"I'm listening."

"Not here. Could we go somewhere—"

"Mom!" Trey barreled through the door and slid to a stop at Leandra's side, his words tumbling out in a breathless rush. "Robby asked me to spend the night. Can I, Mom? Huh? Can I, please?"

Laughing, Leandra turned to her son. "Slow down a minute and start over."

Frustrated, Trey took a deep breath and slowly enunciated each syllable. "Rob-by-asked-me-to-spend-the-night." Then he rushed to add, "Can I, please?"

Todd leaned around Leandra, a smile building on his

face. At last he would meet the one-armed bandit—the indomitable Trey with the broken arm. His smile slipped as he watched Leandra ruffle her fingers through the boy's dark brown hair, the same color as his own. He lowered his gaze to study the boy's face. It was a mirror image of his own at that age, with the same steel-gray eyes, the same Roman-shaped nose, the same cleft in his chin. Leandra's voice sounded as if it came from a thousand miles away as he heard her say, "I guess so. If it's all right with Robby's mother."

"It's fine with me," Ellen said as she pushed through the still-swinging door. Trey let out a whoop and dashed around Ellen as she continued, "We'll probably—"

Todd slid off his bar stool, interrupting his sister. "I've got to get back to the hospital." He shoved his gift into Ellen's hands as he brushed past her. "Tell Robby I'll see him later."

Ellen saw the stricken look on her brother's face. "But Todd, you just got here."

He didn't answer. He was gone, the flapping of the kitchen door evidence of his quick departure. The two women stared at each other in surprise.

"Now what do you suppose got into him?" Ellen asked as she dropped the present onto the tiled bar beside the birthday cake.

Two blocks away, Todd steered his Jaguar to the curb. His breathing was ragged, and perspiration dotted his upper lip. He gripped the steering wheel tightly in his hands, every muscle in his body tensed in denial . . . yet, in his heart he knew it was true.

Hitching up one hip, he tugged his wallet from the back pocket of his slacks. He quickly flipped through the collection of photos until he found the one he sought. A family picture. Over twenty years old. His mother sat in a Queen Anne–style chair, and his father stood behind her. A teenaged Ellen, wearing braces on her teeth, stood at his mother's left, and ten-year-old Todd at her right.

The likeness was uncanny. Unlike Trey's, in the picture Todd's hair was cut in a flat top, but the nose, the cleft chin. . . . It was like looking in a mirror.

His hands shaking, Todd opened the wallet wider and thumbed through the bills until he found the faded check. He slipped it out and studied the date, mentally counting back the years in his mind and guessing at Trey's age.

Dropping his head against the proof in his hands, Todd slumped against the steering wheel. *Why?* he screamed silently. *What had he ever done to deserve this wicked twist of fate?* He fell back against the seat and stared unseeing out the windshield of his car as the answer hit him full force. It was true. A son did truly suffer the sins of his father.

When at last he thought he'd found love, it was only to discover that the son of the woman he loved was his own half-brother.

"Oh, Leandra," he murmured, tears burning behind his eyes. He wanted to protect her, to love her, to care for her always. But he knew he could never see her again. Too much lay between them, things he couldn't erase.

His lips curled into an angry sneer as he threw his wallet against his own reflection on the windshield and jerked the car into gear. Well, Robert Stillman might have thought he had escaped the responsibility of his actions by simply writing a check, but Todd was determined to make his father pay. The debts were long past due.

Todd's anger built as his car quickly ate up the miles between Oklahoma City and Tulsa. Leandra's admission that she had lost her job and been forced to move out of John's house multiplied his anger. What would she do now? How would she manage to support herself and Trey? Before, while living with John, she'd had him to rely on. But now . . .

Todd had never been a violent person, but at the moment he knew he'd take great pleasure in rearranging his father's face, and if Robert Stillman refused to honor his responsibility to Leandra and Trey, that's exactly what Todd was prepared to do. Leandra might never be his to love and care for, but there was one thing he could do for her. He could see that she would never have financial worries.

Robert Stillman had destroyed more lives than Todd cared to count, and today was judgment day.

The tires on his car squealed as Todd wheeled into the driveway of his father's condominium. Once only an investment, the condominium in Tulsa had become his father's home when his parents had divorced seven years before and his father had moved his business's headquarters to Tulsa.

Allowing his anger to carry him, Todd ignored the doorbell and pounded on the door with his fist, then dug his hands deep into the pockets of his slacks and waited impatiently for his father to appear. When the door opened, Todd wasn't prepared for what he saw.

The years hadn't been kind. His father's hair, once rich and dark like Todd's, was now salted heavily with gray. The man whose shoulders had once seemed sturdy enough to carry the weight of the world were somewhat stooped, and the blotchy redness covering his father's neck and cheeks told Todd more than he needed to know about the level of the man's blood pressure.

He steeled himself against the emotions trying to eat

away at his anger. He owed Leandra this confrontation, and for her sake he'd see she got her due.

The surprise that had widened his father's eyes when he'd seen Todd standing at the door disappeared, and Todd watched them narrow in suspicion.

Todd was the first to speak, his voice taut and unforgiving. "Aren't you going to invite me in?"

Robert stepped back. "You don't need an invitation, Todd. My home is yours."

Todd strode past him, ignoring the ludicrousness of his father's statement. He had never set foot in his father's condominium and, after their visit today, never intended to again.

At the entrance to the living room, Todd stopped short. Above the fireplace hung a large oil version of the same family picture Todd carried in his wallet. Scattered along the heavily carved mantel were family pictures taken through the years, each ensconced in a silver frame of varying designs. It seemed his father had suddenly developed a strong sense of family.

One picture in particular caught Todd's attention. Unbidden, he moved to study it at closer range. It was a picture of himself dressed in a graduation gown, his cap dipping rakishly over one eye while he stood with one arm draped around his mother's shoulders and the other around Ellen's.

He remembered the day well. His graduation from medical school. Wesley had taken the picture of the Stillman family—minus, of course, Robert Stillman. His father hadn't appeared for Todd's graduation from medical school, not that Todd had wanted him there. For a moment he wondered how his father had come in possession of the picture.

"What brings you here, Todd?"

Todd whirled at the unexpected nearness of his father's voice and found his father standing directly behind him, watching him covertly. Anger bubbled up from the wound that had festered deep inside Todd for more years than he could remember.

Never taking his eyes off his father's face, he replied in a tight voice, "I met an old friend of yours. Leandra Gallagher. Remember her?" He watched his father's face pale.

"Yes. I remember her."

"I met her son, too. *Your* son."

"So that's what this little visit is all about." Shaking his head regretfully, Robert turned and walked to the bar and poured himself a Scotch straight up. "Join me?" he asked, glancing over his shoulder at Todd.

Remembering his father's attraction to alcohol, Todd replied, "No, thanks."

After he downed the drink, Robert poured himself another before turning back to Todd. "The boy's not mine. He—"

Todd cut off his father's words with a wild gesture of his hand. "Save it, Dad. I've seen the boy. He's yours all right. There's no denying he's a Stillman."

Robert sat down in a cream-colored leather chair, resting his glass on its arm. "No, there's no denying he's a Stillman."

"And that's exactly why I'm here. You've shirked your responsibility long enough. I don't expect you to marry her—Leandra deserves better—but you can damn sure pay child support."

"I've offered her money before, and she wouldn't take it. What makes you think she'll take it now?"

"She's lost her job and her home. She has a lot of

pride, but I think she'd accept your help if it was directed to Trey.''

Robert lowered his gaze from his son's piercing eyes to the glass resting on the chair arm. His hand shook slightly, making the Scotch slosh against the sides of the crystal tumbler. He looked up at Todd. "Exactly what does this woman mean to you?"

Todd's lips thinned to an angry line. "That's none of your damn business."

"You're right, of course, but your feelings for her will weigh heavily on my decision."

"Whatever feelings Leandra and I might have had for each other were destroyed when I discovered her son is my half-brother."

"He's not your half-brother."

"Would you stop denying him, damn it!"

"He's *your* son, Todd. Not mine."

Todd threw up his hands in a gesture of disbelief. "Do you think I'm a fool? I only met Leandra a little over a month ago."

"I've seen her twice over the past eight years."

"Once was obviously enough."

Robert ignored his son's sarcasm. "The first time was the day she came to my office trying to locate you. The second time was the day Trey was born." He lifted his glass and took a healthy drink, grimacing slightly as the alcohol burned down his throat. "Have you ever wondered how the boy got the name Trey?" He didn't wait for an answer. "It's a nickname derived from the fact that he is the third. You were right when you said Leandra has a lot of pride. By law she couldn't give Trey his father's name, but she gave him what part of it she could. She—"

"Todd!"

Todd wheeled at the sound of his mother's voice.

Shocked, he looked from her smiling face to his father, then back to her. It was too much. Seeing his father after an eight-year separation, listening to his father's lies about Leandra, then seeing his mother in her ex-husband's home. It was simply too much.

Without a word to either, Todd bolted from the room, slamming the front door behind him. He had to get away from this madness before it swallowed him whole.

His mother caught up with him at his car. "Todd, wait." Her face was creased in worry. When Todd refused to look at her, Marian Stillman touched her hand to her son's arm. "Please, Todd. Try to understand."

He turned to her, his face flushed in anger. "Why, Mother? For God's sake, why? Didn't he hurt you enough the first time?" He jerked away from her and slammed the car door. The tires squealed as he peeled down the driveway, leaving his mother standing in the front yard, her fingers pressed against trembling lips.

All the way back to Oklahoma City, Todd's mind whirled with the day's events—seeing Trey, confronting his father, seeing his mother and father together after all the years of pain and separation. There was simply too much to absorb at one time.

He forced himself to calm down. In an attempt to find some sense of order, he blocked out all but that which dealt with Leandra and Trey.

The boy was a Stillman. That much was sure. But he as Trey's father? Impossible! He'd never laid eyes on Leandra until that damn Bachelor Auction. Yet something in his subconscious niggled at his certainty. He hadn't known her, had he?

Suddenly he remembered the look she'd given him when she had introduced herself at the auction, almost as if she expected him to know her. Then he remembered their time in Ixtapa and the first time he had kissed her. There had been a familiarity in their response to each other, one he hadn't thought much of at the time. At last his mind carried him to the night they had made love in his home. The fit of their bodies, the rhythm of their lovemaking . . . Could he be Trey's father? Every cell in his being denied the fact, yet for some reason he couldn't explain, he was hesitant. A part of him wished it were true; another part adamantly denied the possibility.

Well, there was one way to find out. Leandra. She wouldn't lie to him. She'd tell him the truth and give him the evidence he needed to nail his father and make him pay.

Leandra wandered around the apartment picking up Trey's toys and putting them away. A dull ache throbbed at her temples, and she rubbed at it distractedly. Twice she had called Todd's number and gotten his answering service. Both times she had left messages for him to call her. She was tempted to call again, but his answering service had assured her he would receive her messages. There was nothing for her to do but wait.

She glanced at the clock on the kitchen wall and willed its hands to move faster. Now that she was ready to put all her deceptions behind her, she was anxious to talk to Todd.

To take her mind off Todd and the clock whose hands refused to move, she pulled out a sweatshirt dress she'd bought for herself and her box of fabric paint tubes. Knowing the bright yellow dress was better suited to Ellen's coloring than her own, she sat down at the kitchen table and began to sketch a design. Within minutes she was so absorbed in the project, she forgot all about the time and Todd's expected call.

When a knock sounded at the door, she glanced at the clock and saw that it was almost eleven. Cautious now that she lived alone, she peeked through the peephole and was relieved to see Todd standing at her front door.

Quickly she slid back the safety chain and yanked open the door. "Thank goodness you got my message. I called twice, and your answering service didn't know where to reach you, but they . . ." Her words trailed off as Todd stepped out of the shadows and into the triangle of light cast from her doorway. His face was pale, and anger tightened his features. Concerned, she drew him into her apartment, "Is something wrong? Todd, what's happened?"

He shook off her arm and faced her, his eyes as hard as tempered steel. "I went to see my father. He told me I was Trey's father. Is that true?"

Stunned, Leandra gasped, "Your father said that? But why?"

"He said that and more. What I want to know, is it true?" When she continued to stand, staring at him in shocked silence, he grabbed her by her upper arms and shook her. "Is it? Tell me, dammit."

"Yes," Leandra whispered.

Todd's fingers slipped from their tight grip on her, and his arms dropped to his sides as he stepped back, shaking his head in denial.

"No!" he railed at the ceiling as he swung away from her. He curled his hands into tight fists and slammed them against his sides. "No. No. No!" he yelled.

He swung back to her, his face a mask of torment. "How? I'd never even seen you before the auction."

"The lake party. Eight years ago. You were drunk. You—"

The memory came, blurry and indistinct, and along with it a guilt too heavy to sustain. "I . . . I raped you. Oh, my God." He sank into a chair and leaned his head back, balling his fists over his eyes.

Leandra dropped down to her knees at his feet. She grabbed his hands and attempted to pull them away from his face. "No, Todd. It wasn't like that. Oh, please listen. You didn't rape me. I gave myself to you. You would never hurt me. I knew that then, and I know that now." Tears rolled down her face as she pleaded with him. "When I discovered I was pregnant, I didn't know how to get in touch with you. I knew you were from Oklahoma City, but the only listing in the telephone directory was your father's business."

Todd continued to mumble denials throughout Leandra's impassioned pleas. She didn't know if he heard her or not. But she had to get through to him! She must! His strength was greater than hers, and she gave up trying to pull his hands away from his eyes and grabbed at his shirt, tugging at him.

"Todd, listen to me! I love you. I was wrong not to tell you before about Trey. I see that now. But I couldn't risk it. He's so young. He wouldn't understand if you left again. I had to be sure of your love for me before I involved him. Don't you see?"

Sobbing now, Leandra released her hold on his shirt and dropped her hands uselessly to her lap. Her head bowed, hot tears streaked down her face, staining her dress in dark wet circles. The futility of her situation overtook her, filling her with remorse. If only she had told him from the first about Trey, maybe Todd would understand. But now . . . now it appeared it was too late.

Leandra's soft crying finally penetrated Todd's anguished mind. Slowly, he pulled his hands from his eyes and looked down at her where she knelt at his feet. The raven blackness of her hair glistened in the subdued light from the kitchen. He wanted to touch her hair, to bury himself in its thickness, but he knew he had no right. After all, he was his father's son. He had inherited the one black trait from the Stillman side of the family he'd always feared would surface. A trait he'd seen in his father and uncle and had heard stories of from as distant as his great-grandfather. But one he had always consciously fought within himself.

An abuser of women. Not in the physical sense, but an abuser all the same. Stillman men used women for their own selfish pleasure without regard for the needs or feelings of the women. Isn't that what his own father had done? Hadn't he seen the effects of that abuse in his own mother's life?

The sound of Leandra's gentle sobbing ripped through him like a jagged knife. God, how he despised himself! He couldn't stand to see her bowing at his feet like some kind of servant. He leaned toward her, raising her chin with the pressure from one finger. She lifted her face, exposing tear-filled eyes. In them he saw a memory. No, he didn't remember Leandra, but he did remember a beautiful raven-haired girl in whose arms he had found peace from the demons that had haunted him and a love he had so desperately needed to believe in again.

On that fateful night eight years ago, he had run from the sight of his father's betrayal, determined to drink away the memory of his mother's stricken look. Then he had met Leah. Not Leandra, but *Leah*. She had been compassionate, understanding, and in her arms he had sought a renewal of life and of love. She had given, and he had taken. And in the end, he had left her with his seed.

"Trey is mine then."

She nodded, tears still streaming down her face.

"And you named him for me?"

Again she nodded.

"Does he know?"

"No. Bits and pieces, but not the whole story."

Todd rubbed his hands up and down the length of his thighs, fighting for control, for a sense of sanity he feared he'd never know again. "Does anyone else know?"

"Only your father. . . and John."

"Why didn't you take the money Dad offered you?"

"Because I didn't go to him for money. I only wanted you."

If possible, her answer shamed Todd even more. "Then why did you call him when Trey was born?"

"I thought you should know you had a son. Unfortunately, your father disagreed. He—"

"That son-of-a—"

Leandra stilled his outburst with a touch of her hand. "Please don't hate him. He only had your best interests at heart. But I wanted something else, too. Something only your father could give me at the time." She took a deep shuddery breath before she continued. "I wanted your name. I didn't want Trey's birth certificate to read 'father unknown.' He put his own name as Trey's father."

Todd stood and pulled Leandra to her feet. Immediately, he dropped her hands and pushed his own deep into his pockets. He had to get out of there, away from her so he could think straight.

Without a word of explanation, he walked to the door, then turned to her, his voice husky. "I'll come back in the morning. We'll talk then."

## NINE

For hours Todd simply drove, winding his way through Oklahoma City's dark streets, his mind a blank. An occasional car passed, blinding him with the beam of its headlights. He hated the lights. In the darkness, it all became a nightmare, something he would wake from. But the lights brought reality, stark and intrusive.

It was late, and he knew he should be home in bed, but he couldn't go there. Not yet. There were too many things to think about, too many decisions to be made. In his bed would be reminders of Leandra and the night they'd made love there. Angrily, he wheeled the car in a sharp U-turn and headed for his office, the one spot in his life she hadn't touched.

Ignoring the light switch by the door, he weaved his way through the dark waiting room, past his receptionist's desk, and to the hallway beyond. At the door to the laboratory, he stopped to fill his senses with the familiar odor of antiseptics and disinfectants. This was his life, the one he had chosen. The one constant in a world suddenly turned upside down. He stepped inside.

Hidden below the cabinet on his left, a solitary fluorescent light glowed. Test tubes and beakers were lined up beneath it, and in the light's ultraviolet iridescence, they shimmered like fine crystal while the stainless steel doors above them gleamed a burnished silver. A sense of order prevailed over all. And that is what he sought—order out of chaos.

It didn't come.

He eyed the locked cabinet on his right, visualizing the neat rows of labeled prescription medicines it contained. Pills to dilate the vessels of the heart. Tablets to reduce inflammation of an incision. Antibiotics to fight infection. Even capsules to control pain.

Nothing for him. No medicine to take for the guilt which burrowed deep within him, eating away at his soul. Nothing to salve the fracture in his own heart.

Heaving a sigh, he turned his back on the laboratory and walked down the hall past the examining rooms to his office. He switched on the desk lamp and collapsed into his chair, leaning his head against the cool leather upholstery. His thoughts continued to spiral in a chaotic mass. He squeezed his fingers against the bridge of his nose and closed his eyes to ease the pounding in his head.

His world—the one growing in his mind and heart ever since he'd met Leandra—was crashing down around him, and he didn't have the power to stop it. For the first time in his life, he had fallen in love. And now it felt as if his heart was being ripped out of his chest.

He opened his eyes to the framed certificates hanging on the wall to his left. Degrees from the University of Oklahoma and Duke University, certificates from his residency and internship, board certifications in general surgery and thoracic surgery, his memberships in medical societies. He knew everything there was to know about the human heart . . . except how to keep it from breaking. Tears welled in his eyes.

*Leandra*, his mind cried. *Leah*, his soul answered. Leah with the long raven hair cascading to her waist. Leah with eyes the color of the purest aquamarine stone. Leah who had given him her love so innocently and so wholly. Leah whose warmth had chased away the chilling memory of his father's transgressions.

Leah. Leandra. The names burned in his mind until at last they fused into one. Leandra. Why hadn't he recognized her from the very first? The answer came fast. He couldn't remember because he'd been drunk and hurting and wanted nothing more than to forget what he'd witnessed at his father's house.

He'd never even asked her last name.

The morning after the lake party, he had awakened alone and with a terrific hangover. His first thought had been that Leah had been a dream, a product of his inebriated mind. Reality or dream, he wanted to find her. He searched, but every lead had come to a dead end. And then he'd gone away to school.

He slammed his fist against the top of his desk, the lamp rocking precariously before settling upright. "It's not fair, dammit!" he raged against the silent room, recalling Leah's disappearance from his life and his father's intervention.

But no matter in how many directions he cast the blame, the responsibility ultimately came back to him. The Stillman Curse. He'd spent half his life hating his father because of it, and now it seemed he was no better than the man he'd condemned.

He'd seen how his mother had suffered at the hand of the man she loved. He wouldn't put Leandra through that kind of hell. He'd messed up her life once. He wouldn't allow himself the opportunity to do it again.

His voice dropped to a whisper as he lowered his head to his crossed arms on the desktop. "It's just not fair."

Throughout the long night, Leandra clung to hope. Todd was upset . . . and understandably so. She put herself in his place and tried to imagine how she would feel if the situation had been reversed. Shock. Anger. Hurt. Guilt. Disillusionment. She knew each of the emotions she had seen ravaging Todd's usually laughing face was justified. She would have felt them all and more.

Her only hope rested in his love for her. She knew it was there. She had seen it, tasted it, and shared it . . . but she had never heard it voiced. That one thought continued to nag at her, making sleep impossible.

Morning came, and when she answered Todd's knock, the last bit of hope seeped out of her. He stood, his face a closed mask, cold and unforgiving at her doorstep. Without waiting for an invitation, he brushed past her and headed for the small dinette table in the breakfast nook.

"I've thought the situation over, and after talking to my lawyer this morning, I've made some decisions." He paused, waiting for Leandra to sit before taking the chair opposite her. When he looked across at her and saw the dark shadows beneath her eyes, he had to force back the urge to take her in his arms and comfort her. Instead, he balled his hands into a tight fist on the table. "I want to adopt Trey."

Leandra's eyes widened in surprise. Moments ago, when she'd seen him at the door, she had been sure it was over, that Todd wanted no part of her or his illegitimate son. Tears of joy welled in her eyes as she stretched her hand across the table to cover his. "Oh, Todd, I can't tell you how worried I've been. I was sure you would never forgive me for keeping Trey from you. And now—"

His voice sliced through hers, silencing her. "I don't think you understand. I'm offering adoption. Not marriage."

The verbal punch knocked Leandra back against her chair, stealing her breath and leaving her speechless. A set of keys hit the tabletop and slid toward her, quickly followed by a brown leather checkbook.

Todd knew he had to do this fast and get out before he changed his mind. "Here are the keys to my house. You and Trey can move in at your convenience. The checkbook is yours. My receptionist will send you a signature card from the bank. It shouldn't take more than a couple of days for the changes to be made. In the meantime—" he tossed several large bills onto the table "—this should tide you over."

Leandra sucked in a deep breath, fanning the flames of anger building inside her until they cauterized the wound he had inflicted on her heart. "No!" she screamed as she raked her hand across the table, sending the keys, the money, and the checkbook flying. "I will *not* be bought. Not by your father, and not by you."

Too late Todd realized the tactlessness of his actions. His voice was calm and patient as he attempted to reason with her. "I'm not trying to *buy you*, Leandra. When you lived under John's protection, you had the benefit of his home and the amenities it offered." He waved an arm, taking in the small, scantily decorated apartment in one full sweep. "You and Trey are accustomed to more than this."

Leandra's chin lifted proudly. "It may not seem like much to you, but Trey and I are quite happy here."

"And you would be even happier in my home. Trey

would have other children to play with, a fenced backyard to play in, and—"

"We will *not* live with you and that is final."

Todd's shoulders sagged in frustration. "I'm not asking you to live with me. I'm *giving* you my house. I'll find an apartment somewhere for me."

The added rejection inflamed her more. "I don't want your house, with or without you. All my life I've been dependent on someone else. First my parents, then John. I'm on my own now. This apartment, whether it meets your standards or not, is Trey's and my home. We are *not* moving."

"Fine," he snapped. "But the checkbook is yours."

"I don't want your money."

"I only want to take care of my son."

"*Your* son? Since when did he become *your* son?" The outrage in Leandra's voice demanded an answer, but she didn't wait for one. She was wound tight and spinning crazily out of control. "Trey is *my* son. I gave birth to him, and I cared for him without any help from you."

The reminder of his father's betrayal twisted Todd's mouth into a bitter frown. "Through no fault of mine."

"Maybe not, but the fact remains, Trey is *my* son, a Gallagher, not a Stillman."

"A point I intend to change when I adopt him. He'll have the Stillman name and—"

"No!" Unable to sit any longer, Leandra sprang from her chair. "Think about Trey and his feelings. How do you think he'll react when you waltz in and announce you are his father and plan to adopt him? Have you considered him at all in any of your planning?"

"Yes. I know it might be difficult at first. But I think he'll understand eventually."

"I disagree. In the last few months, Trey has had to

deal with leaving the only home he has ever known and the loss of John, who was like a grandfather to him. For God's sake, Todd, Trey is only seven! How can you possibly think he could handle suddenly being confronted with a father who is a complete stranger to him?''

Slowly Todd dragged his gaze from the accusation in Leandra's eyes and leaned over to gather up the keys, checkbook, and money from the floor. Pensive, he gathered the bills into a neat stack on the table while he sorted through the tangle of thoughts crowding his mind.

She was right. The boy's emotions must be considered above all else. The child had been through a lot and didn't need another change in his life right now. Todd had seen Trey only once, but that didn't matter. He was his son. And Todd wanted more than anything to make up to him all the time they had lost.

Wearily, he slipped the bills inside the checkbook. ''All right, we won't tell him right away. I'll spend time with Trey. Once he gets to know me and feels comfortable around me, then we'll tell him.''

Leandra rolled her eyes. ''Most seven-year-old boys do *not* have thirty-year-old playmates. So how do you plan to spend time with him?''

Todd glanced up, a plan slowly building in his mind. ''Through you.''

''Me!''

''We'll continue to date, and—''

''No,'' her denial was wrenched through gritted teeth. ''I will not—''

''You will. It's the only way. And we won't be alone. Trey will always be with us.'' He stood and slipped the keys into his pocket, carefully avoiding Leandra's gaze. ''I don't intend to waste any time. Enough has been wasted already. We'll go to a movie tonight. I'll pick the two of you up at seven." He moved to the door to leave, but Leandra's voice stopped him, his hand on the knob.

"You forgot your checkbook."

He turned his head to look at her, meeting the frosty challenge in her gaze. "The checkbook is yours." Before she could argue, he added, "For Trey's use." He closed the door behind him, blocking the sight of her anguished face.

John closed the heavy front door behind him and dropped his suitcase to the floor. In the silent house, the thud echoed hollowly.

"Leandra? Trey?" He listened a moment, half hoping he would hear Trey's answering call.

They were gone. He'd expected it. *Hell, he had demanded it,* he remembered angrily. He should be glad Leandra had obeyed his edict.

His shoulders drooped disconsolately as he bent to pick up his suitcase. He wasn't glad; there was no use denying it. He shuffled up the stairs, but on the landing, instead of taking a right toward his own room, he turned left.

At Trey's door he stopped and peered in. The room was empty and the walls were bare. He swallowed hard, pushing back the wad of emotion rising, and moved on, halting at Leandra's bedroom door.

He looked in, closed his eyes, and looked again. His suitcase slipped from his fingers. Mamie's bed—the one she had willed to Leandra—stood exactly where it had stood for the last twenty years.

Across the top of the mattress were spread Mamie's mink jacket and mink stole. He crossed to the bed and fingered the rich fur. *Why hadn't Leandra taken them?* he wondered. He dropped the sleeve of the jacket and picked up the small box that lay beside it. He thumbed open the lid. Diamonds blinked up at him.

He sank down on the bed, snapping the lid back in place. The jewelry, the furs, they were Leandra's to take. Mamie had given them to her. Unexpected tears burned behind his eyes as he realized the strength of Leandra's pride. Pushing his glasses to his forehead, he rubbed a shaky hand across his eyes.

What he'd done, he'd done for her and the boy. He'd give her until Christmas. If things weren't resolved by then, he'd make them come back. Pushing to his feet, he picked up his suitcase and closed the door. His steps were leaden as he shuffled back down the hall to his own room.

The animated rabbit twirled into the air, his ears twisting into knots and his feet flapping while the dour-faced human beside him watched in disgust. In the silver-white glow cast from the movie screen, Leandra sneaked a look at Todd's laughing face and then at Trey's matching one. Oblivious to her discomfort, the two continued to munch popcorn, sip soft drinks, and laugh at the antics of Roger Rabbit, totally at ease with one another.

She slumped down into her chair, glaring irritably at the screen. She didn't want Trey to like Todd. If he did, then she would be forced to share him with Todd, thereby making Todd a permanent fixture in her life, an occurrence she wasn't emotionally prepared to deal with at the moment . . . or at any time in the near future, she thought petulantly.

Knowing full well the futility of her emotions, Leandra clenched her hands in her lap and willed the jealousy away. Rationally, she knew Todd had a right to see his son. But there was nothing rational or normal about his methods.

She sensed someone staring at her and turned to find Trey watching her, a puzzled frown knitting his brow. Concerned, she leaned across Todd, inadvertently drawing his attention to Trey as well when she whispered, "What's wrong, Trey? Does your tummy hurt?"

He shook his head, then glanced up at Todd before looking back at his mother. "I thought people on dates were supposed to hold hands and stuff." His loud whisper echoed in the quiet theater. Embarrassment flooded Leandra's face as she caught the amused glances of the people sitting behind them.

Where Todd found the humor in the situation was beyond her, but she felt the rumblings of his laughter through her shoulder pressed at his chest. Ignoring Trey's questioning look, Leandra sank back in her chair.

Todd patted her arm consolingly and whispered in a voice tinged with amusement, "It's okay. I'll take this one." He leaned over to Trey and held up his drink in one hand and his popcorn bucket in the other. "That's true, but as you can see, I've had my hands full." He bent over and dropped the bucket to the floor, momentarily blocking Leandra's view of her son. Shooting a warning glance at Leandra, he laced his fingers through hers and pulled her hand to rest familiarly on his thigh before he turned back to Trey. "That better?"

Trey smiled and settled back in his chair. "Yeah."

*For whom?* Leandra thought resentfully as she stared at the bright screen. Flecks of heat crawled up her arm as Todd's thigh muscles tensed beneath her hand. Memories of those same muscles, damp with perspiration and taut with desire, drew a mist to her eyes, making the characters on the screen fade to a colorful blur.

*This isn't going to work*, she thought in desperation.

She tried to ease her fingers from Todd's grasp, but he tightened his hold, refusing to release her hand.

Forty-five grueling minutes later, light flooded the theater when the credits played on the wide screen. At last Todd dropped her hand to help Trey ease his cumbersome cast through his jacket sleeve. For Leandra, it was like being freed from a straitjacket.

But her sigh of relief died on her lips when she stood and Todd draped an arm across her shoulders as he angled her through the crowd toward the exit door. The action, she knew, was for Trey's benefit, but it grated against her already strained nerves to feel the possessive weight of his arm.

During the short drive home, Trey and Todd rehashed the movie, laughing at their favorite lines from the Toon Town characters. Leandra sat, her lips pursed, resenting their easy camaraderie. By the time they reached her apartment, her resentment had grown until she thought she would smother under its weight.

At the door she pasted on a smile as she turned to Todd, blocking his entrance. "Thank you for taking us to the movie. It was fun." She stepped inside, expecting Trey to follow. When he didn't, she turned to him. "Hurry up, Trey. I'm sure Todd is freezing."

Trey looked up at Todd, his eyes questioning, "Aren't you going to kiss her goodnight?"

Todd couldn't help smiling as he squatted down eye level with Trey, only just beginning to realize all he'd missed in not watching his son grow up. "Am I?"

Trey nodded vigorously.

Stealing a glance at Leandra's incredulous face, Todd asked, "Do you think she'll let me?"

"Sure," Trey encouraged. "Girls like that mushy stuff."

"Well, in that case . . ." Pressing his hands against his thighs, Todd pushed himself up to stand in front of Leandra. "I wouldn't want to disappoint her."

Leandra steeled herself for the kiss. Todd's lips touched hers briefly, impersonally, then disappeared. She might as well have placed the door between them for all the feeling he had put behind it.

"How was that?" Todd asked as he moved to let Trey pass by.

"Okay, I guess. Maybe you'll get better with practice."

Leandra's mouth fell open. And since when had her seven-year-old son become an expert on kissing? "No more soap operas for you, young man," she lectured as Trey shrugged off his coat and dropped it to the floor. "Your coat does not belong on the floor. And it's way past your bedtime."

"Ah, Mom."

"No arguments. Now scoot."

Trey picked up his coat by its sleeve and dragged it behind him as he scuffed down the hall to his bedroom. While Leandra's attention was centered on Trey, Todd eased through the still-open door and closed it softly behind him. "You've done a terrific job raising him. He's a great kid."

When she didn't reply, Todd dug his hands deep in his jeans pocket and nervously jiggled change. "Leandra, I know this isn't easy," he began.

"No, it's not." Without ever looking at him, she peeled off her coat and jerked a hanger from the entry hall closet. "And if tonight is any indication, it isn't going to get any easier."

She slammed the closet door and turned on him. "Just exactly what do you want from me?"

"My son."

The longing in his voice was enough to cool her anger. Almost. "Well, you can't have him."

"I didn't mean that the way it sounded." Todd trailed behind her as she stormed to the kitchen. "I just want to get to know him."

She leveled grounds into the coffeemaker and plugged it in, then brushed past Todd to pull a mug from the cabinet, ignoring him.

When she swept past him again, he latched onto her arm and spun her around to face him. "Will you please talk to me?"

She jerked free of his grasp, her eyes sparking in defiance. "I'm not some little wooden puppet whose strings you can pull whenever you need a response. I'm a woman, and I have feelings."

"And what's that supposed to mean?"

"It means holding hands and kissing were not part of our deal. I agreed to act as a buffer between you and Trey—not to act like your lover. Unlike you, I cannot turn my emotions on and off at will."

*So that's what this is all about*, Todd thought as he leaned back against the Formica counter and folded his arms across his chest, watching and listening to the frustration build in her. And she was wrong—dead wrong—if she thought this was easy for him. Holding her hand, feeling her pulse quicken beneath his palm, tasting the passion flare on her lips. No, it hadn't been easy for him either. But it was necessary.

"If the arrangement doesn't suit you, we can end it now." He straightened and turned in the direction of Trey's room. "We'll just tell him the truth."

Leandra caught him by the elbow before he'd taken two steps. He narrowed a glance at her hand, and she immediately dropped it to her side. "No." She sighed deeply in resignation. "No, we can't tell him yet."

Weeks passed. Leandra gave up trying to invent excuses to evade Todd's requests for dates. If anything, he was persistent, and Trey didn't help at all. It seemed as if the two of them had teamed up against her. She could fight Todd, but she couldn't fight both Trey and Todd. The two were becoming fast friends.

Todd, Trey, and Leandra—the three musketeers, she had irritably labeled them. They went to movies, football games, and the Oklahoma City Zoo. Todd had even insisted on accompanying them to Dr. Greenwold's office to have Trey's cast removed.

Leandra found the outings tolerable, because she could fade into the background and let the activity itself command the attention of both Todd and Trey. But the evenings spent in her apartment were unbearable. Preparing and sharing meals as if they were some kind of family. Sitting with Todd on the sofa and holding his hand while Trey perched at their feet and watched television, keeping a watchful eye on his mother and her date. It was driving Leandra crazy.

A couple of days before Thanksgiving, Todd stepped into the kitchen where she was preparing hamburgers and surprised her by asking, "Why don't you and Trey go with me to Ellen's house for Thanksgiving dinner?"

Immediately, Trey jumped up, forgetting the video game he'd been playing in the living room. "Neat! Could we, Mom? Please?"

Leandra silently cursed the thin walls of the apartment as she tore her gaze from her son's pleading face to glare at Todd. But her words were directed to Trey. "Have you forgotten, Trey? We always go to your grandmother's house for Thanksgiving."

"Couldn't we miss just this once? Please, Mom?"

"Your grandmother always looks forward to our coming. You don't want to disappoint her, do you?"

Todd saw the tautness of Leandra's expression and the pout building on Trey's. Scooping Trey up, he tossed him laughing into the air. "I'll bet your grandmother makes the best homemade pumpkin pies in the whole world. We wouldn't want to miss that, now would we?"

*We!* Leandra whirled from the oven to stare at Todd in disbelief as he lowered Trey to the ground.

"You mean you'll come to Grandmother's with us?" Trey asked, his eyes bright with excitement.

Todd ruffled his son's hair. "Sure." He turned a hopeful smile to Leandra. "That is, if it's all right with your mother."

And what could she say with both of them looking at her that way? She turned her back on them and angrily stabbed at a hamburger patty, flipping it under the broiler. "It's fine with me," she mumbled irritably.

Thanksgiving Day at the Gallaghers' home meant two things in healthy proportions: football and food. And usually in that order. All the Gallagher boys had played football in high school. Two of them even went on to play college football at the University of Oklahoma. Any time the family gathered, a person could count on a rousing game of touch football.

Such a game was already in progress on the front lawn when Todd wheeled his Jaguar onto the rock drive that led to the Gallaghers' home. The house itself stood back from the road, partially hidden by a grove of cedar trees. The original structure was banded by a wide porch with a waist-high railing. As the family had grown, so had the house, and additions jutted off from each side, giving the house an odd geometric shape.

When Todd pulled to a stop behind a battered pickup, Leandra jumped out of the car, followed by Trey, and was quickly surrounded by her family.

Todd watched all the hugging and kissing and carrying on from the relative safety of the drive. While Leandra passed from one set of arms to another, Todd studied the house Leandra had grown up in, the one she'd described to him. She hadn't tried to gloss over the condition of her family's home. The peeling paint and sagging front porch were there as she had described. For some reason, it had seemed important to her that he understand her family's financial status. Why, he wasn't sure.

He turned in time to see Leandra step in front of an older man. She grinned up at the man, the gleam in her aquamarine eyes matching his. "Hi, Pop."

Her father eyed her a moment, rubbing thoughtfully at his chin. "Now let me see . . . Leandra, isn't it?"

"Oh, Pop." Leandra threw her arms around his neck, burying her face against the accustomed scratchiness of his cheek before she leaned back far enough to gaze lovingly into his face. "I've missed you."

He eased her arms from around his neck and said, his voice gruff with emotion, "Not enough or you'd have been home for a visit." He cleared his throat as he hugged her to his side and headed toward the car. "Now where are your manners, girl? Introduce us to your young man."

The reminder of Todd brought a wave of guilt. Another lie, another deception. And to her own family yet. Forcing a smile as they approached Todd, she stepped from beneath the weight of her father's arm and aligned herself with Todd. "Pop, I'd like you to meet Todd Stillman.

Todd, my father, Joseph Gallagher. And this," she laughed as she gestured to the group pushing and shoving for a closer look at her *young man*, "is my family. Family," she continued, "I'd like you to meet—"

Wiping the flour from her work-roughened hands, Agnes Gallagher stepped out onto the wide front porch in time to hear her daughter complete the introduction, "—a friend of mine, Todd Stillman." Unlike to the rest of the Gallagher clan, the name was familiar to Agnes. Her fingers tightened in the folds of her apron when the name registered, and she heard again the voice of Trey's school principal. *Todd Stillman is my brother-in-law. The man your daughter is with in Mexico.*

While Agnes watched, Trey walked up and angled himself between his mother and Todd. Agnes's gaze flicked from Trey to Todd, then back again, carrying the features of one and matching it to the face of the other. In the span of a heartbeat, the secret her daughter had carried for so many years unfolded before her eyes.

Leandra spotted her mother on the front steps and waved at her, smiling broadly. At the same moment, Trey saw his grandmother and barreled toward her, while Leandra and Todd followed at a more leisurely pace. Agnes opened her arms, and Trey fell into them, burrowing deep for a hug.

Agnes squeezed him tightly. "Oh, how I've missed you. Let me see that arm."

Trey held out his arm for his grandmother's inspection. "Just like new. You can't even tell it was broken. The doctor told me I could keep the cast, but Mom made me throw it away because it stunk."

Agnes laughed, a laugh as rich and deep as Leandra's. "I'll bet it did. Can you play football yet?"

"Sure I can."

A worried frown creased Leandra's forehead. "I don't know, Trey."

"I'll keep an eye on him," Todd offered as he stepped up and placed a hand on Trey's shoulder. He extended the other to Leandra's mother. "I'm Todd Stillman. I appreciate your allowing me to impose on your family's holiday."

His smile was open and friendly—and so much like Trey's. Agnes wondered if any of the other family members had noticed the resemblance, then blotted the thought from her mind. It was Leandra's secret, and no one would question her. In a family the size of the Gallaghers', one learned early on to honor the privacy of others. Leandra would tell them in her own good time.

"Our children's friends are always welcome in our home." Agnes returned his smile, nodding her acceptance of him. "You two boys run on and play while Leandra helps me put the food on the table."

It didn't take long for Todd to realize he was out of his league when it came to playing football with the Gallaghers. One flying tackle from Jimmy, Leandra's youngest brother, was evidence enough. It didn't seem to matter that they were supposed to be playing *touch* football, not tackle. When the ball was passed to Todd, his offensive players seemed to disappear, and the opposing team's defense came in for the kill. Todd suspected this must be some kind of test and was determined to pass it. If they knew the truth of his relationship with Leandra, he thought ruefully as he lined up for yet another scrimmage, they'd probably beat him to a pulp.

When Leandra called for everyone to come and eat, Todd breathed a sigh of relief.

"Good game, Todd." Joe, Jr. clapped Todd on the back as he passed by him, nearly knocking Todd to his knees. Joe, Jr. glanced back and smiled. "Better hurry. If Jimmy gets to the table before you, there won't be anything left to eat."

Leandra overheard the warning and laughed as she called back, "You mean before you, don't you, Joe?"

Todd climbed the porch steps and sagged against the weathered railing beside Leandra, breathing heavily. "Why didn't you tell me I was offering myself as a living sacrifice to the All-American team?"

Leandra smiled sweetly. "And let the boys miss out on their fun?"

# TEN

The Gallaghers' dining room table stretched from one end of the small room to the other, barely leaving enough space at each end for a person to pass by without either bumping the person sitting there or scraping a shoulder against the wall. Todd chose to scrape the wall as he followed Trey to their seats, carefully avoiding the head of Joseph Gallagher.

Opposite Todd and above the antique sideboard hung a picture of *The Last Supper*. Ironically, the Gallagher table held the same number of chairs.

The dining table itself sagged slightly in the middle, whether from age or from the weight of the food piled on top, Todd wasn't sure. There was enough food to feed an army . . . or maybe even the Gallaghers, he thought as he glanced around the crowded table.

Steam curled from bowls and long casseroles, filling the room with a smorgasbord of tempting aromas that made Todd's mouth water in anticipation: fresh green beans with tiny pearl onions, sweet potatoes buried under a mound of creamy marshmallows, corn swimming in a sea of butter, platters of thickly sliced turkey and ham. And those were only the dishes within his reach!

At the opposite end of the table, he saw two heaping bowls of cornbread dressing, cranberry salad, fruit salad topped with thick whipped cream, mashed potatoes—

His mental inventory was interrupted when Leandra's mother swept by with a basket filled with hot rolls. He closed his eyes, savoring the smell of warm yeast before it was swallowed up by all the other tempting aromas.

Agnes seated herself at the opposite end of the table from her husband. Immediately, a silence fell over the room.

"Everyone join hands." Agnes waited, her gentle smile touching each family member as hands met and clasped on the tabletop.

In Todd's right hand rested his son's small one, and in his left, Leandra's. Never had Todd felt more a sense of family than at that moment.

For the past eight years, Todd had spent Thanksgiving in hospitals pulling double shifts so that other residents and interns could be home with their families. His own family had been over a thousand miles away. But it had been more than miles that kept Todd from going home for the holidays. After his parents' divorce, holidays had lost their appeal.

As he glanced around the table, he wondered if the Gallaghers appreciated what they shared. For some reason, he doubted it. Most people didn't until they'd lost it.

Satisfied that the unifying link had been made, Agnes nodded to her husband. "Joseph, you may bless the food now."

Every head bowed as Joseph murmured a prayer of thanksgiving to God for another bountiful year and for each family member present. With his own son's small hand clasped warmly in his, Todd swallowed hard, silently adding his own thanks for the special blessing he'd received that year.

When the amen sounded, the bevy of voices rose again. Bowls were quickly passed around the table, and plates were filled amid a constant flow of teasing laughter.

Joseph turned to Todd, raising his voice to be heard over the others. "What do you do in Oklahoma City, Todd?"

"I'm a doctor, specializing in thoracic surgery."

Trey's head shot up. "My dad's a doctor, too."

Leandra choked on her tea. A bomb could have been dropped in the center of the table and left less of an impact. Every hand froze while every head turned to stare first at Trey, then at Leandra . . . and lastly at Todd.

Leandra felt her family's scrutiny and understood their shock. Since the day she had told her parents she was pregnant and had refused to name the baby's father, the subject had never been discussed again.

Seeing the thunderous look in her older brother's eyes, Leandra grabbed a bowl from the table in front of her and shoved it at Joe, Jr. "More dressing?" she asked. Though her voice was bright and cheerful, the look she gave her brother begged for his silence. He accepted the bowl silently, but his narrowed gaze said *later*.

Thankfully, later never came. Leandra made sure of it. Throughout the rest of the day, she avoided being alone with Joe, knowing if he pressed her with questions she couldn't lie to him anymore.

Dusk was settling over the countryside when Todd headed the car back down the gravel drive. Trey sprawled out on the backseat with the earphones of his tape player pressed at his ears and a book propped against the door. Leandra knew he shouldn't try to read in the waning light, but she bit back the warning, knowing full well that within five minutes he'd be asleep anyway.

Exhausted, too, from the day with her family, Leandra slid down in her seat and tipped her head back against the headrest.

Todd glanced at her. "Tired?"

"Beat." She kicked off her shoes and stretched her feet out, massaging one foot against the other.

Todd adjusted the rearview mirror and chuckled softly when he caught a glimpse of Trey in the backseat. "He's already asleep."

"Good. Now I don't have to worry about his eyes." At Todd's puzzled look, she added, "He was reading in the dark." She closed her own eyes, shutting out the image of Todd beside her and focused her mind on the hum of the wheels on the highway. Gradually, the soothing sound lulled her into a half-sleep.

"I like your family."

"That's nice," she murmured sleepily.

Accepting that he would soon be, for all practical purposes, alone in the car, Todd twisted on the radio dial and scanned until he found a classical station to keep him company. Violins rose in a crescendo, then fell to a soft diminuendo as Todd set the cruise control at fifty-five and relaxed back against his seat.

Without thinking, he looped his fingers through Leandra's and pulled her hand to his thigh, thrumming their joined fingers in accompaniment with Bach's *Allegro*.

Instantly, Leandra was wide awake. "I don't think the hand holding is necessary. Trey is asleep."

Glancing down, Todd saw their clasped hands and

quickly shook free, moving his hand to grip the steering wheel. "Sorry," he mumbled. "I guess it's habit."

Leandra leaned back and closed her eyes. "Thank God. I'd hate to think it was anything more."

The venom in her voice pulled Todd's gaze from the road to stare at her. "And what's that supposed to mean?"

"Nothing." Wearily, she repeated, "Absolutely nothing."

"Well, it certainly sounded like something to me."

Leandra inched down in her seat, folding her arms protectively at her waist. "It was a rotten day, okay? I'm just tired."

"Rotten day?" Todd looked at her in disbelief. "I thought it was super! Your family was terrific, the food was delicious. What more could you ask for?"

"My life back the way it was."

"Fine. All we have to do is—"

"Tell Trey," Leandra finished for him.

"Right."

"Wrong. It's too soon."

"For who? Trey? Or you?"

The challenge in his tone snapped Leandra's self-control, which had been hovering at breaking point all day. She jerked upright. "Me? This farce can't end soon enough to please me. Did you see the expressions on my family's faces when Trey said his father was a doctor?" Unwanted tears welled in her eyes, and she swiped at them angrily. "They know absolutely nothing about Trey's father. How do you think I feel lying to my parents?"

"If it bothers you so much, why don't you just tell them the truth and get it over with?"

"Right. And which one of my brothers would you like to take on first? Believe me, they've been waiting for this showdown for years. Especially Joe, Jr."

"Why do you insist on worrying about what *your* family will think? How about mine? *My* parents have never even seen their grandson. And what about me? Have you ever considered my position? Hell, Leandra, I have a son in the backseat who doesn't even know I exist. I missed out on the first seven years of his life, and that's something a simple confession can never correct. You, meanwhile, have missed nothing and stand to miss nothing for the rest of his life. Have you ever wondered what might happen when we *do* tell him the truth? What if he decides he doesn't like the idea of a father suddenly appearing in his life and refuses to have anything to do with me? Where does that leave me, Leandra?"

Todd's question haunted Leandra throughout the weekend—a weekend in which Todd was conspicuously absent. She suspected his absence was due to her request for her life to be the way it was. Guilt plagued her. She hadn't been fair. All her concerns had been centered on Trey and on herself. Not once had she considered Todd's position or feelings.

While she wallowed in her guilt, Trey sulked. He moped around the apartment, stretching Leandra's already frayed nerves to the breaking point by continually asking if Todd was coming over.

By Sunday afternoon, she couldn't take any more. She picked up the phone and dialed Todd's number. At his husky hello, her stomach did a backward flip, and she admitted—if only to herself—that she, too, had missed him.

"Trey and I were wondering if you'd like to come over for a while."

"Why?"

His caustic reply confirmed Leandra's suspicions. He

wasn't going to make this easy for her, that was for sure. "To play cards or something." She turned her back to Trey's eager face as she whispered, "Please."

Seconds ticked by while Leandra waited in tense silence.

"I'll be there in a minute."

Leandra sagged against the wall.

Trey nudged his way around her to look up at her. "Is he coming?"

Leandra gave Trey a distracted pat before she replaced the receiver, wondering if she'd done the right thing. "Yes. Go wash your hands and get out the deck of cards."

"Do you have any kings?"

While Todd fanned through his cards, he felt Trey's gaze and glanced up. Trey was staring at him, a frown furrowing his brow. Todd wiped his hand across his mouth self-consciously. "Do I have mustard on my mouth or something?"

Trey blushed and looked down at his cards. "Nah, I was just watching to see if you had any kings."

Todd pulled out two. "Are you cheating or what?" he asked Trey as he tossed the cards across the table.

"Nah." Trey smiled proudly. "I just got a good memory." He tipped his hand, revealing the other two kings. "I win. Want to play again?"

Todd dropped his cards to the table and rocked his chair back on two legs. "I don't think Go Fishing is my game. How about a little stud poker?"

Leandra glanced up from the sweatshirt she was painting and frowned at Todd. "I don't think so."

"Just wanted to see if you were paying attention."

Todd dropped his chair to all four legs again. He gathered up the cards and began to shuffle.

Leandra noticed the weary movements of his hands and the dark circles beneath his eyes and wondered if the reason for his absence throughout the holiday weekend was that he'd been on call. "I think that's enough cards for tonight." She screwed the lids onto the tubes of paint and gathered up her brushes as she stood. "You have school tomorrow, Trey. It's time you were in bed."

"Ah, Mom."

Before Trey could argue further, Todd stood and stretched his arms high above his head. "Come on, champ. I'll tuck you in."

The tug of resentment was instantaneous. The bedtime ritual was Leandra's special time with Trey, a ritual that they had developed together over the years. Leandra's chin lifted defiantly. "Trey can tuck himself in."

Already halfway across the room, Todd stopped and glanced back at her. "I'm sure he can. But tonight he gets some help."

The challenge in the set of Todd's mouth and the sadness she saw in his eyes silenced her objections. She had had Trey to herself for seven years. How could she deny Todd this one night? Turning her back on the two of them, she carried her brushes to the kitchen while Todd followed Trey down the hall.

Through the thin walls, she followed their movements, listening to their mingled laughter as Todd helped Trey prepare for bed. Water ran in the bathroom sink, muffling the sound of Trey's garbled voice as he continued to chatter away while he brushed his teeth. A toilet flushed, then she heard Todd's murmured goodnight as he closed Trey's bedroom door.

Not wanting to appear as if she'd been eavesdropping,

Leandra twisted on the faucet and washed out her paint-brushes.

Todd stopped in the kitchen doorway. "I'll be going now." He turned to leave.

"Todd, wait." Leandra rested her wrists on the edge of the sink and squeezed her eyes shut, gathering the strength to offer an apology long overdue. "I'm sorry."

"For what?"

"Everything. All weekend I've thought about what you said on the way home Thursday night. I know I've been selfish and cranky. I don't mean to be. It's just that . . . well—" She ripped a paper towel from the dispenser and rubbed it over her hands as she searched for the words to explain her position. "—It's all so awkward."

"I know."

The hopelessness in his voice ripped through Leandra. He had loved her once. She knew he had. And he loved Trey. Together they could make a family, if only Todd would allow it. A sob rose in her throat. "Oh, Todd, couldn't we—"

Before she could finish, he had her in his arms, crushing her against his chest. "Don't, Leandra. Please don't say it."

The pounding of his heart against her breasts convinced her she was right. Determined to make him admit his love, she tossed aside her pride. "Before you found out about Trey, you cared for me. I know you did. We could have that again if only you'd—"

His fingers dug into her scalp as he dragged her face to his, silencing her with his lips. He groaned his denial against her mouth, yet his lips sent a conflicting message. They moved across hers, tasting, biting, nipping. He wanted her. She could taste the desire on his lips.

With that knowledge burning deep within her, Leandra

gave herself to him, melting against the hard wall of his chest. Abruptly, he pulled away, his chest heaving as he fought for breath. He dropped his hands to his sides and slowly backed away from her. "No, Leandra. I messed up your life once. I won't let it happen again. You deserve better."

The front door closed, and Leandra sagged over the sink, covering her face with her hands. *Better than what?* she cried silently. There was no man any better suited to her than Todd Stillman. But how would she ever be able to convince him of that?

"What happened to you?"

Trey winced as Leandra touched a tentative finger below his eye. "I got in a fight at school."

"With who?"

"Billy Tolliver. He was making fun of me."

"Fighting is not the way to solve a problem, Trey. You know better," Leandra said sternly.

"But, Mom, he was saying mean things about me. He said I was hatched instead of born like everybody else."

Leandra thumbed away a tear from her son's face, carefully avoiding the purplish swelling beneath his eye. "Now why would Billy Tolliver say a thing like that?"

" 'Cause I don't have a daddy."

Grabbing her son by the shoulders, Leandra held him firmly in her grasp, forcing him to look at her. "You *have* a daddy, Trey."

"Not like the other kids."

Leandra's control snapped. She stood, bracing her hands against her hips. "That's the last straw. Get in the car, Trey. We are going to solve this little problem right now."

With Trey huddled sullenly against the passenger door, Leandra jerked the car into gear and sped away, her fingers tapping an angry staccato against the steering wheel. When she braked to a stop in front of an office building, she grabbed her purse and ordered, "Follow me."

Trey trailed behind her, through the door and across the empty waiting room. Leandra pointed to a chair. "Sit right there and don't move. I'll be right back."

She walked to the receptionist's window. "I'd like to see Dr. Stillman, please."

Mrs. Roulf smiled politely. "I'm sorry, Dr. Stillman isn't seeing any more patients today. Perhaps I could make you an appointment." She flipped open her appointment book and scanned the page. "He has an opening tomorrow at—hey, wait a minute," she called to Leandra's back. "You can't go in there."

It was too late. Leandra was already halfway down the hall. She saw the door marked "office" and didn't bother to knock before she barged in. Todd was sitting with his back to her, studying an X ray through the light from the window behind his desk.

"Todd—"

He wheeled his chair around at the sound of her voice. Mrs. Roulf rushed into the room, stepping around Leandra and blocking her from Todd. "I'm sorry, Dr. Stillman. I told her you weren't seeing any more patients today."

Eyeing Leandra warily, Todd said, "It's all right, Mrs. Roulf. I'll handle this."

As soon as the door closed behind his receptionist, Todd dropped the X ray to his desk and leaned back in his chair. "If this is about last night, I'm sorry. It won't happen again."

Her eyes sparked dangerously at the reminder, but she ignored his apology. "I want you to tell him. Now."

"Tell who, what?"

"Trey! Tell him everything."

"Now wait a minute, Leandra. I said I was sorry. We can—"

Leandra cut him off with an impatient wave of her hand. "This has nothing to do with last night."

"Then maybe you'd better explain what's going on."

Leandra sank into the chair opposite Todd's desk. "Trey was in a fight at school today. This boy was making fun of him because Trey doesn't have a father. I can't stand this anymore, Todd. He's got to know."

It was what he had wanted from the beginning, yet Todd hesitated. Doubts crowded his mind. What if his son didn't want a father? What if he lost that one last link with Trey by telling his son the truth?

He glanced up at Leandra's determined face and knew he had no choice in the matter. Trey would learn the truth one way or another. "All right. Where is he?"

"In the waiting room."

Todd pressed the buzzer on his desk. "Mrs. Roulf, send the little boy in the waiting room to my office, please."

A moment later the door opened, and Trey walked in. He stopped just inside the door and ducked his head.

Todd motioned for Trey to come to him, and Trey reluctantly scuffed his way across to Todd's desk. Pulling the boy onto his lap, Todd tipped Trey's chin up and looked at his eye. "That's quite a shiner you've got there."

"Yeah, it hurts, too."

"Want to tell me about it."

Trey glanced at Leandra. She nodded her head, encouraging him to go on. "This kid said I was hatched because I don't have a daddy, so I socked him one."

Todd fought back a smile. "I see. Did it make you feel better to hit him?"

"Not really."

"Would it make you feel better to know you had a daddy?"

Trey shrugged one shoulder. "I guess so."

Todd took a deep breath. "Well, you do have one, Trey. I'm your daddy."

Trey's gaze remained fixed on his tennis shoes as he said, "I know."

Todd heard Leandra's shocked intake of breath. He glanced at her incredulous face, then back to his son's. "You know? How could you know?"

"Robby told me. He heard his parents talking about it one night."

"Well, why didn't you say something?"

Trey shrugged again. "I thought it must be a secret or something."

"Is that okay with you? That I'm your father?"

"Yeah."

A soft smile formed on Todd's lips. "Well, its okay with me, too. In fact," he glanced up at Leandra, seeking her approval of the offer he was about to make, "if it's all right with your mother, we can change your name to Stillman, and then everyone will know you have a daddy."

Trey glanced at his mother, then back to Todd. "Is Mom going to change her name to Stillman, too?"

Avoiding Leandra's intent gaze, Todd nervously cleared his throat. "No. Your mother's name will still be Gallagher."

"Then I don't want to change mine."

"Why not?"

" 'Cause we match. If I change my name, then Mom and me won't match anymore."

It was over, finally over. But the relief Leandra had expected didn't come. If anything, she was more depressed than ever. Her presence was no longer required for Todd and Trey to be together. The two talked on the phone, made plans, and went places. Leandra was no longer in the picture.

Instead of the three musketeers, it was the dynamic duo. Todd and Trey. Father and son. Pete and repeat. She would have laughed at the irony of it all, but she couldn't. There was nothing funny about the way she felt.

If anyone ever needed a friend, it was Leandra. She needed someone to talk with, someone to help fill the empty hours when Trey was gone with Todd. But for a woman who had spent most of her adult life avoiding close relationships, there were few friends.

With another lonely Saturday stretching out in front of her, Leandra mentally thumbed through a list of possibilities. John came to mind, but the thought was quickly discarded. He had severed their relationship; it was up to him to make the first move to reconcile. She could drive up to visit her family—but no, then she would have to explain Trey's absence, and she wasn't prepared to deal with that emotional scene yet. There were the sweatshirts she was making for Christmas presents that she hadn't finished painting, but she didn't feel creative enough to tackle them.

*Ellen!* The name flashed in her mind like a marquee. Thankfully, Leandra couldn't think of a reason *not* to call her, except, of course, the fact that she was Todd's sister. But Leandra decided not to hold that against her!

An hour later, as she sat nursing a cup of hot coffee at Ellen's breakfast bar, she didn't regret her decision to call. Ellen had a friendliness about her that escaped description. She was open, honest, and at times even downright blunt.

Ellen smiled at Leandra over the rim of her coffee cup. "I guess I should feel bad that I was inadvertently the cause of Trey's discovering Todd was his father.'' She wrinkled her nose impishly. "But I don't."

"It's just as well. Trey had to be told eventually."

Ellen reached across the bar and placed her hand on Leandra's, stilling her nervous stirring. "Something tells me you need a friend with a good ear. Want to talk about it?"

Unexpected tears welled in Leandra's eyes. "Is it that obvious?"

Ellen nodded sagely.

Leandra's shoulders sagged as she lowered her spoon to the saucer. "I feel so left out. For weeks Todd and Trey and I did everything together, and now it's just the two of them. I guess that sounds kind of selfish, doesn't it?"

"Not in the least. There are times when I'm jealous of the time Wesley spends with Robby. And I can imagine it's even worse for you with Todd trying to make up for lost time."

"Trey loves him. But then it would be difficult not to love Todd."

"Aha! So that's the reason behind the blues. You love the jerk!"

Leandra's face flushed a bright red. "He's not a jerk."

"Oh, yes he is. Anybody who lets his past dictate his future is a jerk in my book."

Leandra shook her head. "You don't understand."

Ellen rested her elbows on the table and leveled her gaze on Leandra. "I may not understand everything, but I *know* my brother and all the insecurities he carries around. He's running scared, and it's up to you to knock some sense into his head."

"Now *I* don't understand. The only thing he had to run

from was Trey, and Todd accepted him with open arms.
It's *me* he's running from."

"Wrong." Ellen reached for the coffeepot and refilled
their cups. "You obviously haven't heard about the
Stillman Curse."

# ELEVEN

Even though she was sure she would die at any moment, Leandra pasted on a cheery smile as she fluffed up a pillow behind her head. "Don't worry about me. I'll be fine. Now hurry, or you'll be late for the game. Oh, and Trey," she added before he closed her bedroom door. "Take your key in case I'm asleep when you get back."

"Okay, Mom." Trey pulled the door behind him, and although he didn't slam it as he usually did, the clicking sound made Leandra's head throb even more.

She listened a moment for the sound of the front door closing, then slipped from bed and staggered to the bathroom. Aspirin. She needed an aspirin. And maybe a nap. Then she'd feel better.

The effort it took to cross to the bathroom sapped her strength, and she leaned heavily on the vanity as she pulled open drawer after drawer, rummaging for an aspirin. There weren't any. She sagged over the bathroom sink, pressing her fingers against her temples. Surely she was dying. No one felt this bad and lived to tell it.

She twisted on the faucet and splashed cold water over her face, hoping to cool the fever burning beneath her cheeks. The bleary-eyed woman looking back at her from the mirror made her grimace. She looked nearly as bad as she felt.

On the way back to bed, the room started spinning around her. She grabbed at the wall, sagging weakly against it. When the room grew still again, she eased toward the bed and collapsed onto it. She fumbled for the blanket and pulled it over her head. Yes, she was going to die. No doubt about it.

The lanky center lobbed a ball from midcourt. The ball circled the rim, dipping precariously to the outside before falling into the basket just as the buzzer sounded for the end of the first half. A roar erupted, shaking the stands of Lloyd Noble Arena.

Todd clapped Trey on the back. "Did you see that, son? What a shot!" Todd settled back in his seat and picked up his popcorn bucket and tossed a few kernels into his mouth. He passed the bucket to Trey. "Want some?"

Trey shook his head and glanced at the clock on the scoreboard.

Todd saw the anxious look. "What's wrong, Trey?"

"Nothing. Is the game almost over?"

"No, it's halftime." Todd put his hand to Trey's forehead. "Do you feel sick or something?"

"No."

Trying to get information out of Trey was like pulling teeth, but Todd had sensed his son's lack of enthusiasm throughout the game and was determined to discover the cause. "Do you want to go home?"

Immediately, Trey's face brightened. "Could we?"

"Well, sure. But I thought you wanted to see the basketball game?"

"I do, but I'm worried about Mom."

"What's wrong with your mother?"

"She wasn't feeling too good when we left."

Todd was up and out of his seat, gathering their coats. "Why didn't you say something? We didn't have to come to the game."

Trey ran, trying to keep up with Todd who was taking the gymnasium steps two at a time. Breathlessly, he replied, "She said she was feeling better, but she didn't look so good when we left."

Ignoring the speed limit, Todd raced home, his powerful Jaguar eating up the miles between Norman—the home of the University of Oklahoma—and Oklahoma City. When he reached the apartment, he used Trey's key to let them in.

"You stay here, and I'll go and check on her."

Trey obediently waited while Todd slipped into Leandra's bedroom.

The blanket and sheet were twisted into a knotted ball at the foot of the bed, and Leandra lay sprawled on her back, her eyes closed. Todd tiptoed across the room. When he switched on the lamp beside the bed, Leandra groaned and rolled away from the glaring light.

Leaning across the bed, Todd placed the back of his hand to her forehead. Heat seeped into his hand.

"Leandra?" he whispered, then repeated a little louder, "Leandra?"

She levered herself up on one elbow, then fell back, throwing an arm across her eyes. "Where's Trey?" she mumbled.

"He's in the living room. How do you feel?"

"Like a Mack truck hit me. Do you have an aspirin? My head's killing me."

"No, but I'll get some. Do you need anything else?"

She rolled over and buried her head under a pillow. "A new body," came her muffled reply.

Todd chuckled. "I'll see what I can do."

He eased out of the room and nearly bumped into Trey, who was standing just outside the door.

"How's Mom?"

"Sick. But she'll live. Go pack a bag, and I'll take you to Robby's. You can spend the night with him."

When Trey didn't budge, Todd said, "Is there a problem?"

"If I leave, who'll take care of Mom?"

"I will. Remember? I'm a doctor."

Todd dropped Trey off at Ellen's, then ran by the grocery store and picked up aspirin. Not knowing what other supplies Leandra had on hand, he also grabbed a thermometer, two gallons of juice, and a couple of cans of soup. By the time he returned to the apartment, Leandra's fever had risen measurably.

He unwrapped the thermometer and lifted Leandra's head. She fought him like a wild woman—or at least she thought she did.

"Easy now," he soothed. "I'm just going to take your temperature."

"Where's Trey?" she mumbled incoherently.

"He's at Ellen's. Now open your mouth and hold this thermometer under your tongue."

She swatted feebly at the thermometer. "I'm not sick. Just tired. Give me the aspirin and go away."

"I'll give you an aspirin if you'll be a good girl and let me take your temperature."

She eyed him warily through feverish eyes but opened her mouth and let him slip the thermometer under her tongue. While he waited for an accurate reading, Todd lifted her wrist to take her pulse. She rolled her eyes at him.

As soon as he removed the thermometer, Leandra asked irritably, "Will I live?"

"One hundred and four. Probably. But for the next twenty-four to forty-eight hours you're going to feel like hell."

He popped open the aspirin bottle and shook out two into her hand, then held up a glass for her to drink.

Obediently, she swallowed the aspirin and washed them down with the juice, then fell back against the pillows. A tear squeezed from between her closed lids and slid miserably down her face.

Immediately contrite, Todd sat down on the edge of the bed and smoothed her damp bangs from her forehead. "Don't cry, Leandra. The aspirin will take effect in a few minutes and you'll feel better."

"I'm not crying because I'm in pain," she sobbed. "I'm crying because I'm sick."

Todd chuckled at the absurdity of her statement. She brushed impatiently at his hand while tears coursed down her cheeks. "You don't understand. I don't have *time* to be sick. There's a load of towels in the washing machine that have been there all day. I don't even have the energy to throw them in the dryer, and yet I promised Trey we'd put up the Christmas tree tomorrow." She flung her arm across her eyes.

Todd was speechless. She looked so pitiful lying there in her faded flannel gown, her face flushed with fever and tears streaking down her face. He had never been able to deal with a woman's crying, something his sister Ellen had taken advantage of when they were growing up. Not knowing what else to do, he pulled tissues from the box by the nightstand and pressed them into her hand. "Don't worry, Leandra. I'll help Trey put up the tree."

She wadded the tissues in her hand. "I don't have a tree!" she screamed hysterically. "I don't even have a string of lights to hang on a tree. I'm twenty-five years old, and I don't even own one crummy string of lights." She buried her face against the ball of tissues, sobbing uncontrollably.

It was the fever talking, Todd told himself. Leandra was not normally a hysterical woman. If she weren't so sick, she wouldn't be carrying on like this. Tomorrow she'd regret the emotional display. The best thing to do was let her cry it out . . . in privacy. Slowly he stood and slipped from the room, closing the door behind him.

He stopped in Trey's room and switched on the light. Unlike Leandra's bedroom with its double bed and solitary chair, Trey's room had a finished look, with a bed, a dresser, and pictures on the wall. Cars in bright primary colors raced across the bed's twin-size comforter and continued up the wall, obviously painted there by his mother. *And she'd said she wasn't artistic*, he thought with a rueful shake of his head.

He walked to the dresser and picked up a picture of Trey and Leandra captured while they rolled laughing in the grass. It was probably taken at John's house, judging by the manicured lawn and flowerbeds in the background. He replaced the picture and trailed a finger along the dresser, rubbing it across the smooth leather of a baseball glove lying there. So his son liked baseball, did he? He'd remember that in the spring when it came time for Little League sign-ups. Maybe he could even coach Trey's team.

An unexpected melancholy settled over Todd, and he

dropped down on the edge of Trey's bed, pulling the baseball glove to his thigh. He knew so little about his son. His likes, his dislikes. He glanced around the room, noting the college pennants and life-size posters of athletes.

Even at the age of seven, Trey was showing a strong interest in sports, probably a result of the Gallagher uncles' influence. Would his interest be the same if Todd had been around to influence him?

Irritated by his own futile thoughts, Todd slapped the glove against his thigh as he stood. He couldn't worry about the what-ifs, only the present. And for the present, he'd promised his son he would take care of Leandra and that's what he'd do. And he'd start by relieving some of her worries, no matter how trite they might seem.

In the small kitchen, behind the louvered doors, Todd found the washer and dryer. Sure enough, the washer was filled with wet towels. He transferred them to the dryer and switched it on. The thud of wet towels tumbling against the sides of the dryer echoed hollowly in the quiet apartment. But the rhythmic sound made him feel better. Already, he had alleviated one of Leandra's worries. The others would be equally dealt with.

After picking up Trey's toys from the living room, Todd went to check on Leandra. She had kicked off the covers again. They lay in a snarled knot at the foot of the bed. He pulled the sheet up over her and smoothed a hand across her brow.

Her face, usually porcelain smooth, was blotchy from crying and a fine mist of perspiration dampened her brow and hair. It didn't detract from her appeal. If anything, it made her even more endearing. The tears she'd shed earlier and the glimpse he'd had of what she considered her failings tugged at his heart. This woman was special and deserved more out of life than what she'd been dealt . . . and at his hand.

God, how he missed being with her. For a man who had planned his life around his profession, purposely avoiding intimate relationships, this feeling was foreign and not at all pleasant. Leandra Gallagher had stepped into his life and, in a matter of months, had turned it upside down.

She moaned in her sleep and pushed at the covers. Todd caught her left hand and held it, murmuring soft words of comfort as he pulled the sheet back to her chin. He settled her hand on top of the sheet and started to turn away but quickly snapped back. The rings—the ones she'd worn to stave off unwanted questions—were gone, and only a band of lighter skin hinted they'd ever been there at all.

He knew the rings weren't necessary anymore, not with him there to claim Trey as his own, but their absence bothered him for a reason he couldn't explain. Frowning, he stepped into the bathroom, wet a cloth, and returned to drape it across her forehead.

After she quieted, he pulled a chair beside the bed and sat down, propping his feet on the mattress and rocking the chair back on two legs. The vigil began.

At some point during the night, Todd dozed off, but a sixth sense doctors are blessed with jerked him awake. When he leaned over her to check Leandra, her teeth were chattering. She huddled under the covers, shaking uncontrollably.

"Leandra?"

"C-c-cold," she whispered through parched lips. "S-s-so c-c-cold."

Not knowing where extra blankets were kept or even if she owned any others, Todd went to Trey's room, pulled off the brightly painted comforter and draped it over Leandra, tucking it tightly around her body for maximum heat. Still she shivered.

"So cold," she whimpered.

Without thinking, he kicked off his shoes and climbed under the covers with her, pulling her against his body. Tremors continued to wrack her body as he held her, rubbing his hands up and down her arms.

Long after the trembling stopped and she slept, Todd continued to hold her until he, too, fell into a troubled sleep.

A dull pounding woke Leandra. She touched her hand to her forehead. The fever was gone, but the headache still thumped away. Flat on her stomach, she attempted to roll to her back, but a mound of blankets held her prisoner. She opened one eye to a narrow slit and found the headlights of a bright red car staring back at her. *Trey's comforter? What's it doing on my bed?* she wondered in confusion.

The events of the previous night slowly unraveled—the fever, the blinding headache, and Todd's pushing aspirin at her and forcing juice down her parched throat. *Bless him*, she thought with a sigh when she recalled the chills that had followed the fever and the subsequent warmth of the blankets he had piled on.

Both eyes flipped open wide to examine the empty bed beside her. More than blankets had warmed her, she remembered in surprise. A dream? She closed her eyes again, savoring the memory. No, not a dream. Todd had been there. The memory was too real to have been a product of her feverish mind.

The pounding stopped, and she heard a loud thump followed by a muffled curse. Confused, Leandra lifted a hand to her temple, then realized the sound had not originated in her head as she had thought but from somewhere beyond the bedroom door.

Pushing and kicking at the mound of covers, she rolled to a sitting position, then to her feet. Dizzy, she steadied herself a moment before following the strange sounds to the living room. Todd knelt in the corner by the couch, his back to her, hammering a wooden stand onto the base of a Christmas tree.

"What are you doing?" she asked incredulously.

Todd spun at the sound of her voice, a smile building on his face. "Good morning! How are you feeling?"

Obviously he'd been home, for his face was cleanly shaven and he wore a pair of faded jeans with a sunny oxford shirt tucked into the beltless waistband. He made her feel like a washed-out rag in comparison. She hugged the faded pink roses on her flannel nightgown beneath her breasts as she pushed back her matted hair. "Better. Or at least I think I will be when I get something to drink. My teeth feel like they're wearing woolly socks."

Todd chuckled as he stood, pulling the tree upright. "There's orange juice in the refrigerator." He stepped back and appraised the tree. "Looks straight to me." He glanced back at Leandra. "What do you think?"

"It's beautiful, but—"

"I know," he said eyeing the tree critically and purposely ignoring the train of her thoughts. "It lacks something."

"No, I wasn't criticizing. I—"

He held up his hand, stopping her. "Don't say another word." He picked up a sack and pulled out a string of colored lights. "Lights. That's what it needs." Ignoring her flustered look, he guided her toward the kitchen. "Get your juice, then come sit on the couch and direct. I've never been any good at stringing lights on a tree."

Convinced she was still sleeping and this was all a
dream she would wake from at any minute, Leandra
poured a glass of juice and walked back into the living
room. She had to step over a pile of carefully folded
towels to reach the couch.

*Towels!* She stared at them and then at Todd. He was
perched on a chair, weaving lights through the tree's
branches. "Did you dry and fold these towels?"

Todd glanced back over his shoulder at the pile of towels, then turned back to the tree. "Yeah."

"Why?"

"They were wet. Now do you think we need another
string around the top, or is one enough?"

It was just towels and it probably hadn't taken more
than ten minutes to fold them, but Leandra felt the most
ridiculous urge to cry. "One is fine," she replied absently,
not caring whether he hung one or twenty. She settled
back against the couch, curling her feet beneath her as she
marveled at the change in him.

In all, seven strands of lights were woven through the
spruce's thick branches at Leandra's direction. When Todd
finished, it was past noon. "I'll bet you're hungry," he
said as he jumped down from the chair.

"A little. I'll make us something." Before she could
stand, Todd was pushing her back down to the couch.

"I'll get it. Hope you don't mind canned soup. I picked
up some last night at the grocery store."

Unaccustomed to being waited on, Leandra sank back
down in surprise. "Canned is fine," she murmured as he
disappeared into the kitchen.

*Why is he doing this?* she wondered in confusion. *And
why is he being so nice?* From the moment Todd had
learned he was Trey's father, his relationship with her had
been strained at best. And since Trey had been told the

truth . . . well, there hadn't been a relationship. And darn it, even considering all the rejection he had piled on her, she *still* wanted a relationship with him. But just thinking about the futility of it all made her head ache again.

Unbidden, Ellen's words came to mind. *He's running scared, and it's up to you to knock some sense into his head.* Scared? Of what? Ellen had claimed it was the Stillman Curse. She had been quick to add that she didn't believe it, of course, insisting the curse was a product of Todd's imagination. Oh, she had admitted to the Stillman men's infidelities all right, but she had vehemently denied Todd's assumption that he would be just like them.

Could it really be something within himself that kept them apart and not some fault he had discovered within Leandra? The possibility had merit.

Knock some sense into his head, huh? As weak as she was, Leandra knew she had the strength to deliver a powerful wallop. She smiled to herself as Todd returned with a tray of soup and crackers. *Beware, Todd Stillman,* she thought smugly. *Before the day is out, you're the one who'll be nursing a headache because I'm about to knock the daylights out of you.*

Leandra ate a little of the soup, then excused herself, saying a shower would surely make her feel better. Todd watched the gentle sway of her hips as she crossed the room, and he felt a tightening in his chest. He assured himself that *any* woman dressed in a faded flannel nightgown and wearing bright red socks on her feet would affect him similarly.

He slumped down on the sofa and stared at the empty hallway morosely. If, for some reason, he ever lost the use of his hands and could no longer perform surgery, he knew he could turn to the stage. After the performance he'd given this morning, he was sure he'd be a success. Smiling and laughing and talking when he'd have rather pulled the blanket over his head and ignored her—his own blanket and in his own bed, he added.

Being around Leandra only made it more painful to accept the fact that he couldn't *be* with her—at least not in the sense he wanted.

The pipes hidden behind the kitchen wall groaned when Leandra turned on the water in the bathroom, jarring Todd from his thoughts. Gathering up the bowls, he headed for the kitchen and began to clean up the mess he'd made.

Trey. He'd call Ellen, then go and pick up Trey. Trey would act as a buffer between him and Leandra, taking some of the pressure off Todd.

In the bathroom, Leandra squirted a scented shower gel on her washcloth with a liberal hand. She chuckled as she rubbed the cloth across her body. Leandra Gallagher was no fool. She knew Todd was putting on an act, and the knowledge gave her the strength needed to deliver a performance of her own, one he wouldn't be able to resist.

After stepping from the shower, she quickly dried her hair and fluffed it around her face. A little blush and a touch of lipgloss were added to disguise the telltale signs of the illness she'd suffered the night before. Satisfied with the results, she headed for her closet. She rummaged through it, discarding hanger after hanger until her hand rested on the black sweatshirt dress she'd worn the day of Robby's birthday party—the same day Todd had learned he was Trey's father.

Moments later, when she stepped into the kitchen, Todd was just hanging up the phone.

"Wes is taking the kids to a matinee and for pizza afterward. Ellen will call us when they get back."

"Oh? That's too bad." Trailing a scent of the perfumed

gel, Leandra breezed by him and stopped at the pantry door. "I was hoping Trey could help us make Christmas ornaments for the tree." She rose to her toes and struggled with a box on the top shelf.

"Here, let me." He stepped behind her and stretched over her as he helped pull down the heavy box. It was a mistake, the first of two. The second one occurred when he sucked in a shocked breath as her buttocks brushed against his groin.

The first mistake had been voluntary, something any gentleman would have done. The second mistake had been mandatory—for Todd, a matter of survival.

Unfortunately, in gulping in the deep breath, he had filled his senses with her seductive scent.

They stood with the box pressed between them, their gazes locked, each aware of the passion dancing just out of sight.

Determined to keep things light, Todd tore his gaze from hers and pulled the box from her grasp. "Where do you want it?"

Leandra stood in the pantry, smiling at his back. "On the floor in the living room is fine." *This is going to be easier than I imagined*, she thought impishly as she followed close behind him.

Kneeling over the box, she pulled out brightly colored construction paper, glue, and scissors. "Have you ever made a Christmas chain?"

"Not since kindergarten."

"Well, surely a surgeon knows how to use scissors." She handed him a pair. "You cut, and I'll glue."

They sat side by side, their backs pressed against the couch. Todd cut strips of paper while Leandra glued the links together. The chain grew as Leandra chatted away.

"I had coffee with Ellen the other day."

She ignored Todd's disinterested grunt and continued happily on. "She was telling me the most fascinating story. About the Stillman Curse. Have you heard it?"

For a fraction of a second, the scissors stilled in Todd's hand, then clicked sharply when he clamped the handles together. A jagged strip of paper fell to his knee, and he picked it up and wadded it into a ball. "Yeah. I've heard it."

"Fascinating, isn't it? Though a bit ridiculous." She slipped a strip of blue paper through a link and squirted a dot of glue on it. "Imagine anyone thinking a personality trait can be passed through genes." She pressed the ends of paper together and then patted Todd's hand before reaching for another. "Of course, I'm sure with your training as a doctor I don't need to tell you that."

Todd dropped the scissors and turned to glare at her, his wrist draped over his knee. "All right, Leandra, what's this all about?"

She looped another paper through the link, avoiding his gaze. "Whatever do you mean?"

"I mean," he said as he clamped his hand around her wrist, stilling her movements, "if you have something to say, say it."

Leandra met his angry gaze squarely, calmly. When a woman had nothing to lose, she could gamble it all. "Okay, fine. I think the Stillman Curse is a bunch of hogwash, something you conveniently hide behind."

The anger was there, flashing in his gray eyes before they turned to a cold, flat steel. His hand tightened on her wrist, but she refused to flinch. "You are not your father, Todd. You cannot allow his mistakes to dictate your life."

He pushed her hand out of his grasp. "Yeah? And what would you know about it?"

"I know this much." She twisted around until she faced

him, her shoulder pressed at his propped knee. "I know that you are kind and loving and gentle. You would never hurt me."

"I already did. Remember?"

"Yes, I remember. And I have no regrets." Her mouth curved in a soft smile as she laid her hand on his arm. "You gave me Trey, and I can never fault you for that."

His arm tensed beneath her fingers, his hands balling into a tight fist. "Don't, Leandra. Don't do this."

"Why, Todd?" Confident, she pressed closer, until her face was only inches from his. "Tell me why."

"Leandra," he warned as he drew back from her.

"You want me, Todd, as much as I want you."

With the couch pressed at his back and Leandra in his face, he was trapped. The control he had clung to all day snapped like a brittle twig, releasing his anger. Grabbing her by the shoulders, he shook her. "Yes, I want you, dammit. But I won't give in to lust."

But even as he uttered the denial, he was crushing her against him, locking her in an embrace she had no wish to escape. "Love me, Todd," she whispered.

His lips closed over hers, silencing her, bruising her with his denial. Yet, he couldn't deny the passion she tasted budding on his lips or the need she felt throbbing beneath his skin.

The gentleness she had credited him with was missing. But gentleness was not what she needed or what she sought. Weeks of suppressed longing demanded a savage release.

Their tongues met and clashed, each seeking to dominate the other. Seconds slipped into minutes and minutes into eternity as the kiss rocked on.

Before Todd's fevered mind could register her deft movements, Leandra had his shirt in her hands and was tossing it aside. But when her fingers found the snap on his jeans, he closed his hand over hers. "No, Leandra."

Ignoring his rasped command, she pulled until the snap gave way.

What little restraint he had left vanished as quickly as his shirt. Leandra had planned to seduce him. But somewhere along the way, she had lost control. The seduction was now his. Hooking a hand under her knee, he dragged her across his lap, bunching her dress at her waist. His hands roamed over her buttocks, fitting her tight against him. It wasn't enough. He wanted to be in her, to possess her.

Stripping the thin piece of silk from her hips, he rolled her to the floor beneath him and buried himself in her. Heat flashed, hot and blinding, as he drew her to the brink. Together, they plunged over the edge, spiraling down until they rested, gasping in each other's arms.

"I love you, Todd."

The words were freely given, but Todd could not accept what he did not deserve.

Still trembling from the effects of their lovemaking, he rolled to his feet and pulled on his jeans. "I'm sorry, Leandra." He grabbed his shirt from the floor and shrugged it on as he headed for the door.

"Todd?" He stopped with his hand on the door but didn't look back. He couldn't bear to see the hurt in her eyes.

Her voice quivered slightly as she whispered, "I have no regrets."

# TWELVE

Leandra braced her hands against the shower wall and let the cold spray wash over her head and run in stinging rivulets down her body. Gradually, it dulled the heat Todd had kindled beneath her skin.

The shame and rejection he had left her with weren't as easily dealt with. She stepped from the shower and rubbed the thick towel over her body, shivering as much from reaction as from the cold.

It was time to face up to the facts. Todd didn't want her, and the sooner she accepted it, the better off she'd be. But even the acceptance didn't take away the hurt.

The doorbell sounded, and she pulled on her robe, tying the belt at her waist as she hurried to answer the door. She sent up a silent prayer that Todd would not be there, that he would drop Trey off and leave without her having to face him.

When she opened the door, she found Ellen standing on the narrow porch, a covered dish in her hands. She was accompanied by an older woman, obviously Ellen's mother.

Ellen lifted a knowing brow. "Something tells me we picked a bad time to drop by."

Self-consciously, Leandra touched a hand to her wet hair. "I just stepped from the shower." Sensing her guests' uneasiness, she added, "But please come in."

As she passed by Leandra, Ellen raised her hands, indicating the dish. "Chicken soup. Mother's cure for everything from the common cold to a broken heart. Where shall I put it?"

Ellen's casual comment about a broken heart sent a stab of resentment through Leandra. Surely Todd hadn't told them about her throwing herself at him? Mortified by the thought, Leandra gestured to the small kitchen, feigning nonchalance. "Just set it on the stove. I'll put it away later."

Marian extended her hand to Leandra. "My children have no manners. I'm Marian Stillman, Todd and Ellen's mother."

Accepting Marian's hand, Leandra smiled weakly. "I'm Leandra Gallagher." Remembering her own manners, she gestured toward the couch. "Please, sit down."

"Thank you, dear." Marian shrugged out of her coat and sat down, smiling at Leandra. "I've heard quite a bit about you."

Ellen breezed into the room and took the seat beside her mother, leaving Leandra no choice but to take the chair opposite the couch. The arrangement made her feel as if she were on trial and they were her jury.

"Not all bad, I promise." Ellen laughed gaily. "Trey has been talking Mother's ear off all afternoon."

"Such a sweet boy. And so concerned about your health. When Todd arrived a bit ago, Trey insisted on a complete update." Marian laughed, the sound a softer version of Ellen's. "I don't believe he quite trusted Todd to care for you, thinking he could do a better job of it himself. He'd be here now, but Todd insisted on taking him to dinner so you wouldn't have to trouble yourself unnecessarily." Marian leaned forward, her brow knitted in concern. "How are you, dear? Are you feeling better?"

"Yes, thank you." How could she have thought them a jury? They were so kind and obviously concerned. Leandra warred with the sudden tears welling in her eyes.

Unfortunately, Ellen saw the telltale glimmer before Leandra lowered her gaze. Never one to beat around the bush, Ellen demanded, "Okay, what's he done now?"

Leandra shook her head. "Nothing. Really. I guess it's just the after effects of the flu."

"Don't worry about Mother, Leandra. She knows Todd's hang-ups as well as I do, so you might as well 'fess up."

Leandra bit down hard on her lip, trying to stop its quivering.

Ellen folded her arms across her chest and relaxed back against the couch. "You might as well tell us. We aren't leaving until you do."

Something told Leandra that Ellen would make good her threat. With a self-conscious glance at Marian, Leandra clasped her hands in her lap. "He doesn't love me. It's that simple. He wants Trey but not me."

"Horse manure!" The crude expression did not quite fit the primness of Todd's mother. "He loves you. He's just too scared to admit it. Todd is haunted by the memory of his father's transgressions." Marian sighed deeply as she patted her daughter's hand. "Ellen, thank God, was spared the horrors that Todd witnessed firsthand. In retrospect, I could have spared Todd that experience." She shook her head sadly. "But at the time, I'm afraid I was having difficulty enough maintaining my own sanity."

Ellen smiled smugly, "I told you she was on our side."

\* \* \*

Though she appreciated Ellen and Marian's attempts to keep her hopes up, as Leandra closed the door behind the two women, she knew Todd was a lost cause. Whatever his reasons, he had rejected her love for him.

It would have been difficult, awkward at best, to face Todd again so soon after his rejection. Thankfully, he spared her the humiliation. When he brought Trey home, he walked Trey to the door, then left, promising to call his son later that week.

After that, it was easy to avoid Todd. Leandra made Trey answer the phone, and when Todd came by to pick up his son, Leandra hid in her room. It was the coward's way out, she knew, but her only means of self-preservation.

Intent on blocking him from her mind, Leandra threw herself into Christmas, baking and shopping and preparing for the holiday ahead. Even that didn't work. When surrounded by shoppers in the crowded department store, she would discover a sweater the color of his eyes. Or while searching through cookbooks, she would find a recipe she knew he would enjoy. The thoughts would come unbidden, sneaking into her mind and leaving her with a sadness so deep it ached.

Everything about the holiday—the brightly colored lights and tinsel, the cheerful music, things she'd once found so much pleasure in—suddenly seemed gaudy and dull. *Would Christmas ever be the same again?* she wondered. *Would anything ever be the same again?*

Three days before Christmas Todd dropped by unannounced. Since she hadn't been expecting him, Leandra opened the door herself. It was the first time she'd seen him since the night they'd made love. The sight of him stole her breath away.

"May I come in?" he asked uncertainly.

Embarrassed by her reaction, Leandra stepped back, opening the door wider. "Of course. Trey isn't back yet. He's gone to a movie with Billy Tolliver."

"I guess that means he's forgiven Billy for saying he was hatched."

Leandra laughed nervously. "Yes. I guess so."

Todd nodded toward the pile of wrapping paper and ribbon scattered on the living room floor. "Wrapping presents?"

"Yes." As she led the way into the small living room, Leandra cleared a path with her foot, pushing the wrapping paraphernalia out of the way. "With Trey out of school, it's difficult to find a private moment to wrap his presents. Would you like to sit down?" she asked.

"Thanks." He pulled off his jacket and draped it across his knees as he took a seat on the couch. "I was hoping to catch you alone. I wanted to ask you about Christmas."

"What about it?"

"When we were at your parents' on Thanksgiving, your mother invited me back for Christmas. I told her we'd probably spend Christmas with my family."

Leandra's eyes widened. "You what?"

"I told her we'd be spending Christmas with my family. Is that a problem?"

"Yes, it's a problem. Trey and I always spend Christmas Eve at home, then go to my parents' on Christmas Day."

"We spent Thanksgiving with your parents."

"So?"

"So we'll spend Christmas with mine."

"We spent Thanksgiving with my family because *you* wanted to spend it with Trey, and at the time he didn't know you were his father. The three musketeer act isn't necessary anymore.''

"Fine. Then Trey can spend Christmas with my family."

"No!"

"Leandra—"

She jumped up from her chair, knocking over a battery-operated robot. "No, Todd. Trey spends Christmas with me."

"He has spent the last seven Christmases with you. It's my turn."

"Why are you doing this to me?" she demanded angrily.

"I'm not doing anything to you, Leandra. I only want to spend Christmas with my son. You are welcome to come to Ellen's with us."

"Oh, and wouldn't that be fun! Me and you and Trey, the perfect picture of family."

"There is no reason to be sarcastic."

"Isn't there? My life was my own before you came back to Oklahoma City. I didn't have to worry about holidays or where they would be spent."

"I think you're forgetting that *you* waltzed into my life, not the other way around. Revenge, wasn't it? Isn't that what you sought?"

Leandra dropped back down in her chair, sulking. "Oh, yes. Revenge. And isn't it sweet?" she said spitefully.

Leandra closed the door behind Todd and Trey and sagged against it. In the corner of the living room, gifts were piled beneath the Christmas tree, their hue changing from green to red to blue, then back again as the tree lights blinked on and off.

Her first Christmas Eve without her son. She didn't

think she could stand it. Gulping back a sob, Leandra pushed away from the door and strode across the room. Angrily, she jerked out the plug. Without the lights, the paper ornaments she and Trey had made to hang on the tree looked as miserable as she felt.

The doorbell sounded. Thinking Trey had forgotten something, Leandra quickly swiped at her tears as she ran to fling open the door.

John stood in the doorway, presents piled to his chin. "Well? Are you going to invite me in?" he asked gruffly.

"John?" Leandra clamped her hands across her mouth, then reached a tentative hand to his sleeve, unable to believe he was actually there. "John, it's really you. Yes!" she laughed. "Yes, please come in." She backed from the door, making way for him to enter.

John dumped his presents beneath the tree and turned to her, pulling her in his arms for a quick hug. "It's good to see you again, Leandra."

She touched a hand to his cheek. "You, too, John."

He peered over her shoulder. "Where's Trey?"

Immediately, Leandra's smile dissolved. "At Todd's."

"At Todd's? Why aren't you with them?"

"How long have you got?"

Frowning, he pulled off a leather glove. "Long enough."

Leandra dropped down on the couch and patted the cushion beside her. "It was as I expected. No. It was worse. When Todd found out about Trey, he decided he wanted his son. Unfortunately, it was not a package deal."

"Damn," John swore under his breath. "My plan didn't work."

"What plan?"

John scrunched his mouth up, frowning at the Christmas tree. "I was afraid you were staying with me out of a sense of loyalty. I figured if I was out of the picture and you didn't have a place to live or a way of supporting yourself and Trey, you would turn to Todd. It looks like my plan backfired."

"John Warner! You conniving old fool."

He lifted his chin a fraction. "I've been called worse."

"And deserved it, I'm sure. Do you realize how worried I've been? Or how much Trey has missed you?"

A smile curled one side of his mouth. "He has, huh?"

"Yes, he has. He'll be sorry he missed seeing you tonight."

"Well, there's always tomorrow."

Leandra grabbed at the suggestion. "Why don't you come over in the morning? You can watch Trey open his presents."

"Can't. I've got plans."

"Plans? On Christmas morning?"

He stood and pulled on his coat. "I'm having brunch with Marge."

"Marge! Marge Harris?"

"Do you know another Marge?"

Leandra laughed, clapping her hands in delight. "No, and I think that's wonderful."

"Humph. Well, don't get any ideas in that pretty little head of yours. It's only brunch."

Ellen breezed back into the living room, her velvet hostess gown swirling around her ankles. "The kids are all watching the Christmas special on television. Does anyone in here need anything?"

Robert Stillman handed his daughter a glass of champagne. "No. Wes has taken care of us in your absence. How about a toast?" He turned to his family and lifted his glass. "To each of you. May you find in this Christmas season the fulfillment of all your dreams."

Crystal clinked as a round of Hear! Hears! echoed in the room. Standing at the fireplace, one arm draped at the mantel, Todd eyed his father warily. Trust once lost was hard to earn back.

Robert stepped beside his ex-wife and placed an arm around her waist, then lifted his glass again. "Another toast."

A premonition of doom tightened Todd's stomach muscles.

When each glass was held aloft, Robert smiled down into his ex-wife's uplifted face. "I've asked your mother to marry me again. And she has agreed. We would like the blessings of our children."

Todd's hand clutched convulsively at the champagne glass. She wouldn't. She couldn't, not after all he'd put her through. Todd felt as if the rug had been jerked from beneath his feet.

"Oh, Mother. Daddy." Ellen's voice broke as she hurried to throw her arms around her parents.

Without tasting the champagne, Todd lowered his glass to the mantel and strode from the room.

In what had once been her husband's study, Marian found Todd staring out the window to the darkness beyond. "Todd?"

The muscles on his back tightened, but he didn't turn around or acknowledge her presence.

"Todd, please." She touched a hand to his sleeve, and he jerked away.

Pulling her hands to her waist, she said, her voice low and patient, "I know it's hard to understand, Todd. Especially for you."

Todd wheeled, his eyes dark and condemning. "How can you do this, Mother?"

"To whom, Todd? To myself or you?"

His face tightened at the implication. He turned from her and glared at the darkened window.

"Sometimes I've wondered who suffered more from your father's deceptions, you or me? When I met Trey, I knew then that you were the one who suffered more. I can't say what your father did to you was right, but he did it out of love."

"Love?" Todd sneered. "You have a warped image of love, Mother, if you think denying a man knowledge of his son constitutes an act of love."

"In this case, it does. Your father didn't want you to have to choose between your dream to be a doctor and whatever sense of responsibility you might have felt toward Leandra."

Todd tensed at the mention of Leandra's name.

"Does it surprise you that I know her name? It might surprise you more to know that I've met her. She's a beautiful woman, Todd, both inside and out. A mother couldn't ask for anyone better to love her son. She does love you, you know."

Todd's shoulder sagged. He pressed a hand to the cold windowpane and rested his forehead in the crook of his elbow. "Yes, I know," he murmured wearily.

"Do you love her as well?"

"It doesn't matter how I feel about her."

"Oh, but it does."

"I'd only hurt her."

"Why?"

Todd lifted his head and laughed, the sound hollow and haunted in the quiet room. "You seem to forget, Mother. I'm a Stillman, remember? We Stillman men have a tendency to hurt the women who are foolish enough to trust us with their hearts.''

''That is the most ridiculous statement I've ever heard.''

''Ridiculous?'' Todd wheeled, anger twisting his face and darkening his eyes. ''I'll tell you ridiculous. I watched you suffer as a result of my father's indiscretions. Hell, I was there the day you found him in bed with another woman. In your own house, Mother.'' The flash of pain in his mother's eyes made him regret the callous reminder. He crossed to her and took her hand in his. ''Listen, Mother, you don't have to marry him again—''

''No, you listen.'' When he would have pulled away from her, Marian tightened her grip on his hand, refusing to release him. ''I've been silent long enough. Your father made a mistake. Several mistakes. But I've forgiven him, and I think it's time you did, too.''

''I won't forgive him. I can't.''

''Yes, you can. He's changed, Todd. If you'd only give him a chance, you'd see that change. It's time you got on with your life and quit living in the past. Your father's mistakes are his to live with, not yours. You have a wonderful son and the opportunity to have a family of your own. Don't lose it, Todd.'' She rose to place a kiss on his cheek, then thumbed away the trace of lipstick she'd left there. ''I love you, Todd. And your father does, too, if you'll only let him.''

Todd stood in the doorway holding Trey in his arms. At Leandra's alarmed look, he hurried to explain, ''He's okay. He's asleep. He wanted to come home.''

Leandra reached to take him from Todd, but Trey tightened his hold on Todd's neck, mumbling sleepily, ''I want Dad to tuck me in.''

Leandra salved the sting of jealousy. Her son was home

on Christmas Eve. She wouldn't let jealousy ruin that happy thought. She stepped back to let Todd pass. Then together, they walked down the short hall to Trey's room.

While he waited for Leandra to pull back the bed covers, Todd eased Trey's coat off, then laid him down, pulling the covers up to his chin. "Goodnight, Champ."

" 'Night, Dad." Trey glanced up at Leandra. "Has Santa Claus come yet?"

She smiled. "No, darling."

"I hope he remembers my puppy."

Her smile drooped. "Trey, I told you Santa couldn't bring you a puppy because the apartment manager doesn't allow pets."

Trey ignored the reminder and rolled to his side, turning his back on Leandra's troubled face. "I think I'm gonna name him Rambo."

Before Leandra could argue the point, Todd draped an arm around her shoulders and guided her from the room, softly closing the door behind him.

In the living room, he dropped his arm from her and gestured toward the Christmas tree. "In the morning when he opens his presents, he'll forget all about the puppy."

Leandra shook her head sadly. "You don't know Trey. When he sets his mind on something, he doesn't forget." She shook off her blue thoughts and turned to Todd, offering him a smile. "Thank you for bringing him home. It means a lot to me to have him here on Christmas Eve."

"It's okay." He gestured to the tree. "Looks like it grew some since we were here earlier."

Leandra chuckled as she, too, looked at the presents heaped beneath the tree. "Yes, it has. John came by."

Surprised, Todd glanced at her. "He did?"

"Yes. He's going to come by again tomorrow to see Trey."

"Have you forgiven him?"

Leandra shrugged. "There wasn't anything to forgive. John did what he thought was best for Trey and me." She sighed heavily. "Unfortunately, it didn't work out quite the way he expected."

"I don't think I'm following you. The man kicked you out of his house and fired you from your job. Surely an apology is needed in there somewhere."

Leandra smiled as she adjusted a glittered paper star on the tree. "Not from John. Even if I had expected it, John's not the type to offer one."

As he watched Leandra straighten the crudely constructed star, Todd thought of Ellen's tree, laden with ornaments collected over the years. The comparison tore at his heart.

"Do you believe in miracles, Leandra?"

She dropped her hand to her side and stepped back from the tree, raising her gaze to the angel perched at the top. Like so many of the decorations on the tree, it had been shaped by Trey. A halo—fashioned from gold braid found among Leandra's sewing scraps and a thin piece of wire—dipped precariously over the angel's head. Black button eyes, one slightly askew, stared down at Leandra.

Did she believe in miracles? Hugging her robe at her waist, Leandra replied sadly, "I used to."

She turned and walked away, leaving Todd standing beside the tree staring up at the Christmas angel.

Toys, opened then quickly discarded, peeked from beneath the wrapping paper and ribbon littering the floor.

"Here's one for you, Mom. From Papa John."

Trey dumped the large package in Leandra's lap, then ducked back under the tree in search of a present with his name on it.

"Now what do you suppose this is?" Leandra asked as she fingered the silver bow on top.

"Probably something dumb, like a toaster or a waffle iron."

"Trey Gallagher! That wouldn't be a dumb present. Especially since we don't have either one of those items." She continued to eye the gift, measuring and weighing it in her hands. Half the fun in getting a present was guessing its contents. "Bigger than a bread box, but smaller than a—"

"Gosh, Mom. Just open it!"

Leandra chuckled as she tore off the red foil paper. "Okay. Okay. Give me a minute."

As she lifted off the box's lid, Leandra's mouth dropped open.

Trey crawled over and peeked into the box. "What a weird present," he said before scurrying back beneath the tree.

Tears welled in Leandra's eyes as she pulled the mink jacket to rub against her cheek. Mamie's coat. Even after so many years, Mamie's scent still clung to it. Leandra had left it at John's when she'd moved out, no longer feeling worthy of the gift.

At the bottom of the box was another smaller gift. Her fingers trembling, Leandra picked it up and opened it. Beneath the layers of tissue, Mamie's jewelry glittered, reflecting the lights of the Christmas tree.

John, sweet John, Leandra thought tearfully. For Leandra, the gift was a symbol of his acceptance and love. He couldn't have given her anything she would have treasured more.

The phone rang, and Trey bolted for the kitchen, calling, "I'll get it."

Leandra carried the jacket to the hall closet to hang it up.

"Neat! What is it?"

With her hand on the hanger, Leandra paused, listening to Trey's conversation.

"Ah, come on. Please? Well, when do I get to see it then? Sure, she will."

"She will, what?" Leandra asked suspiciously as she crossed to the kitchen.

Trey waved her away. "We'll be there in fifteen minutes." He hung up the phone and let out an excited whoop as he hopped around the narrow kitchen. "Santa left me a present at Dad's! I'll bet it's a puppy. I just know it is! Come on, Mom. I told Dad you'd bring me over to get it."

"You *what*?"

"I told him you'd bring me over. Hurry up," he called as he darted for the hall closet, "I told him we'd be there in fifteen minutes."

Leandra stood on Todd's front porch, muttering curses under her breath. If Todd had bought Trey a puppy after she had specifically told him the apartment manager didn't allow pets, she'd murder him. No jury in the world would convict her—especially if she put Trey on the stand. One look at his disappointed face—the one she could already picture when Trey was forced to give the puppy back—and the jury would demand the electric chair for Todd.

The thought of Todd strapped in the electric chair, begging for her mercy, drew a satisfied smile to Leandra's face. *Yes*, she thought smugly, *there is something to be said for justice*.

The door opened and Todd stepped out. "Merry Christmas!" he said as he scooped Trey up into his arms.

"Merry Christmas, Dad." Trey hugged Todd's neck, then leaned back and asked, "Where's my present?"

"Present? What present?"

"Ah, Dad. Quit teasing. The one you told me about on the phone."

"Oh, *that* present!" Todd chuckled as he dropped Trey to his feet. "Well, follow me."

Todd led the way through the house with Trey hot on his heels. Leandra followed at a distance, feeling awkward and miserably out of place. When they reached the kitchen, Todd paused. "Do you hear something?"

Trey and Leandra both cocked their ears. A soft scratching sound came from the other side of the door.

"My puppy!" Trey yelled as he bolted for the door. When he jerked it open, a brown ball of fur tumbled through the opening.

Leandra's chest swelled in anger. He'd done it, exactly as she had imagined. Well, it was up to her to put an end to it before Trey became attached to the puppy. "Trey, you can't—"

"Your mother's right, Trey. Dogs don't belong in the house." Todd scooped up the puppy and guided Trey through the back door. "You can play with him out here, okay?"

Trey accepted the puppy and laughed when it licked his face. "I'm going to call him Rambo. Don't you think that's a good name?"

Todd chuckled. "Perfect. Come inside if you get cold," he added before he closed the door.

"Todd Stillman, I could wring your neck. You heard me tell Trey he couldn't have a puppy, yet you got him one anyway."

Todd lifted his hands palms up. "I didn't get him the puppy. Santa Claus did."

Leandra rolled her eyes, then leveled them at him. "Did you see the size of that puppy's paws? It's going to be as big as a horse when it grows up."

"Not quite that big."

"We cannot have a dog in our apartment, Todd, no matter what the size. Now you might as well go out there right now and tell Trey he can't keep the dog."

"He can keep it here, at my house, in the backyard."

"Will you listen to yourself? That's almost as bad as not having one. Trey couldn't stand not being able to be with his—" She stopped short as she realized Todd's intent. Narrowing her eyes at him, she said, "If you think for one minute you are going to steal Trey away from me, using a puppy as bait, you've got another think coming."

Todd pushed his hands in his pockets and stared at the tile floor. "I'm not trying to steal Trey from you, Leandra. I had more in mind sharing him."

"Sharing him? We are already sharing him, but you're trying to buy his affection by giving him things I can't."

"That's not exactly what I had in mind either." He blew out a long nervous breath. "Maybe if you'd come with me, you'll understand."

Reluctantly, Leandra followed him. At the door to his bedroom, Todd stopped and turned to her. "Remember last night when I asked you if you believed in miracles?"

Confused, Leandra nodded.

"You said you used to. I hope that doesn't mean you don't anymore." He pushed open the bedroom door and stepped back, allowing Leandra an unobstructed view of the room.

In slow motion, she moved her hands to cover her mouth. Todd's bed—the one in which they had made magical love—was gone. In its place stood Mamie's antique four-poster bed. Leandra's gaze darted around the room, taking in the French armoire, the cheval mirror, the chaise lounge, and the dainty vanity with its carved legs and cushioned bench.

Tears brimmed in her eyes as she moved from piece to piece, running her fingers along the familiar warmth of the wood. At the bed she stopped and touched a palm to the rough mattress ticking. "How did you get this?"

She heard his sigh even from a distance of ten feet. "Believe me, it wasn't easy. I had to do some fast talking to get John to let me have it, and then I had to promise Wesley my season tickets to the OU basketball games to get him to help me move it all."

"Why?"

"Well, Wesley drives a pretty hard bargain. He—"

"No, I mean, why did you want the bed?"

Todd shrugged uneasily. "It's your bed. You told me so yourself. I figured you'd want it."

A tear dropped from her cheek and widened to a dark circle on the mattress. She traced the wet spot with the tip of her finger.

Purposely misunderstanding the cause of her tears, he said, "I know," and crossed to stand behind her, placing his hands on her shoulders. "It looks tacky without a bedspread, but knowing how much you love to decorate, I thought you'd rather pick out everything."

Turning into his chest, Leandra cried, "What are you doing to me?"

"I hope proposing."

She lifted her tearstained face to meet his gaze, her eyes wide, not daring to hope. "Proposing?"

"Pitiful, isn't it? But you were warned," he said as he shook a finger in her face. "I told you I didn't know how to court a woman properly."

"But what about the curse?"

"The Stillman Curse? There is no curse." He chuckled. "At least not in the sense I thought. Last night Mother explained to me that the only thing Stillman men seemed to be cursed with is a strong dose of stupidity when it comes to appreciating what they've been blessed with. I only hope I'm not too late."

As usual, Leandra was having a difficult time following his train of thought. "Late? For what?"

"To see a miracle. You do believe in miracles, don't you, Leandra?"

In answer, she threw her arms around his neck, laughing and crying at the same time. "I do believe, Todd. Miracles happen every day."

Her momentum threw Todd off balance, and he fell across the bed, carrying Leandra with him. "Ouch!" he cried as he lifted one hip from the mattress, rolling Leandra off him to land at his side.

"What is it?"

"I almost forgot." Todd reached into his back pocket and pulled out a box. He handed it to her. "Merry Christmas."

Fresh tears welled in Leandra's eyes as she sat up and accepted the velvet box. Her fingers trembling, she lifted the lid. Ensconced in the black satin folds inside, an emerald-cut aquamarine stone surrounded by baguettes blinked back at her.

"Now don't get any ideas," Todd warned. "The ring isn't new. Ellen put it in the jeweler's box because she was afraid I'd lose it. And I know you're probably disappointed because it isn't the conventional diamond engagement ring, but the first time I saw you, I remember thinking your eyes were the same color as grandmother's ring. I knew you were meant to have it."

Clutching the ring box in one hand, Leandra threw her

arms around Todd's neck. "And you said you weren't a romantic," she chided teasingly as she lowered her lips to his.

The spark was instantaneous, catching the tinder of long suppressed need and blazing to full passion. Through the French doors leading from the master bedroom to the patio out back, Todd heard the distant sound of Trey's laughter and the high-pitched yelp of Rambo's bark.

"Leandra?" Todd mumbled against her mouth.

"Hmmmm?"

"How long can a little boy stay outside without danger of freezing to death?"

Leandra chuckled as she flicked her tongue against his earlobe. "Long enough."